# QUEST FOR THE LOST POWERS

## FOUR UNTOLD TALES

# QUEST FOR THE LOST POWERS

## FOUR UNTOLD TALES

KAI and ZANE stories by Tracey West

COLE and JAY stories by Adam Beechen

Random House 🏠 New York

Manufactured under license granted to AMEET Sp. z o.o.
by the LEGO Group.

AMEET Sp. z o.o.
Nowe Sady 6, 94-102 Łódź—Poland
ameet@ameet.eu
www.ameet.eu

www.LEGO.com

Published in the United States by Random House Children's Books, a division
of Penguin Random House LLC, 1745 Broadway, New York, NY 10019, and in
Canada by Penguin Random House Canada Limited, Toronto. Random House
and the colophon are registered trademarks of Penguin Random House LLC.

rhcbooks.com

ISBN 978-0-593-64848-3 (trade)
ISBN 978-0-593-64850-6 (ebook)

Printed in the United States of America
10 9 8 7 6 5 4 3 2 1

First Edition 2023

# CONTENTS

# Prologue

Thank you for coming to visit, friend. If you have time, let us catch up over a fresh pot of tea. Because I have tales to tell you—four tales, to be exact. Four tales that the world does not yet know.

You may have already heard that the last time the ninja faced the Overlord, they lost their Elemental Powers. Kai lost the power of Fire. Cole lost the power of Earth. Jay lost the power of Lightning. And Zane lost the power of Ice.

These four ninja disappeared from the public. But then they returned, with their powers restored. Rumors flew about how the ninja did this. Intense training? Sorcery? A journey to another realm? The rumors became more and more wild, but the ninja remained silent.

Silent to most, but not to me. Today I will tell you the stories, as the four ninja told them. Their journeys were very different, but all of them were filled with danger, adventure, and excitement.

Now then, let's begin, before our tea gets cold. . . .

Master Wu

## Chapter One
# Kai's Lost Spark

It was another busy night at Mr. Chen's Noodle House in Ninjago City. Customers filled every seat in the colorful restaurant, gobbling down bowls of fried rice, puffy potstickers—and the best noodles in the world of Ninjago.

"Look how many noodles I can slurp all at once!"

Kai, the Fire Ninja, leaned over his piping-hot bowl of food and dug in with a pair of chopsticks.

*Slllllurrrrrrrrrrrrrrrrrrrrrrp!*

A few of the customers looked up from their meals to stare at Kai. Meanwhile, on the other side of the counter, the owner of the restaurant, Skylor Chen, sighed.

"It looks like the same amount of noodles you slurped five minutes ago, Kai," Skylor said, brushing a stray lock of dark red hair behind her ear. "Don't you have anything bet . . . *trrr* . . . I mean, something more important to do?"

Kai wiped his mouth with the sleeve of his sweatshirt and frowned. "Um, no more Fire powers, remember? There's *nothing* important for me to do anymore."

Above her, a TV screen was tuned to NGTV News. Veteran reporter Gayle Gossip appeared on the screen, standing on a busy Ninjago City street. In the distance, police sirens wailed.

"Crime in Ninjago City has been rising steadily, ever since word got out that the ninja have lost their Elemental Powers," the reporter was saying. "I tried to contact the ninja for comment, but they're not returning my calls. In this reporter's opinion, they seem to have forgotten who they really are. Powers or not, ninja, Ninjago City needs you!"

Skylor stared at Kai in surprise. "You haven't returned her calls?"

Kai shrugged. "I haven't charged my phone in days," he said. "What's the point? Without my Fire powers, I've lost my spark."

"That's not true," Skylor insisted. "You still know Spinjitzu. You're still as smart as you ever were, and brave. You can still do good in the world."

"Ninjago City has an excellent police force," Kai replied. "They don't need me getting in their way."

Skylor shook her head. "This isn't like you, Kai. Didn't you lose your Elemental Powers once before? You got them back in the Never-Realm, right? Just by digging deep inside yourself?"

"That time in the Never-Realm, I brought my Fire powers back with intense focus and concentration," Kai said. "But I just can't do it this time. I've tried and tried. It's no use."

He slurped down some more noodles to make his point.

Then a voice came from the restaurant's kitchen.

"Skylor! The potstickers are less than puffy again!"

"Coming!" Skylor yelled. She turned to Kai. "This conversation is not over."

*Sluuuuuuuuuuuurp!* Kai ate some more noodles. Then the noodle shop door slammed loudly and a thunderous voice cried out.

**"THE ROTTEN RABBITS ARE IN THE HOUSE!"**

Kai turned to see that three muscled guys had burst into the restaurant. They each wore black eye masks and had long, curly mustaches that looked like whiskers. Their teeth were sharpened into fangs, and blades shaped like rabbit ears extended from their black helmets. On their feet, they wore heavy black boots that looked like big rabbit feet.

"This is a robbery!" the first Rotten Rabbit shouted.

"Give us all your money!" cried the second Rotten Rabbit.

"And be quick about it!" added the third Rotten Rabbit.

Kai sighed. Several gangs of amateur goons had formed when news got out that the ninja had lost their powers, and this looked like one of them. He stood up and faced the robbers. "Why don't you bad bunnies hop back to whatever greasy garden you came from?"

"Who's gonna make me?" the main Rotten Rabbit asked.

"He's Kai, the Fi— I mean, Kai the Ninja!" one of the noodle customers yelled.

The Rotten Rabbit eyed Kai. "A ninja? Really? He looks like a dude in a hoodie with noodle broth stains on it."

A teeny, tiny spark flared up in Kai.

"Oh yeah? I'll show you," Kai said. *"Ninjaaa—"*

"Rotten Rabbits, Hop to it!" the main robber yelled.

*BAM!*

Before Kai could launch into Spinjitzu, the three rabbits all kicked him with their big boots. He soared through the air and crashed into a large fish tank. The tank toppled over onto him, dousing him with water.

"What's going on here?"

Skylor emerged from the kitchen, and her eyes narrowed as she assessed the situation.

"*Hiyaaaaaaaaaaaa!*"

She launched herself over the counter and landed in front of the stunned rabbit robbers. Before they could react, she attacked them.

*BAM!* A powerful leg sweep brought one of the robbers to his knees.

*SLAM!* She grabbed the second robber and flipped him, pounding him into the ground.

*CRASH!* She jumped and delivered a high kick to the main robber, sending him crashing into a table.

Terrified, the robbers scrambled to their feet.

"RUN, RABBITS, RUN!" their leader yelled.

Skylor stepped over the broken table and helped Kai to his feet.

"See what I mean?" he asked. Water dripped from his hair and clothes as he scooped up the flopping fish and put them back in the tank. "I couldn't even take care of a bunch of low-level goons. It's hopeless! Without my Fire powers, I have no idea what I'm supposed to do."

Skylor stared at Kai with a worried frown.

Meanwhile, on the TV screen, Gayle Gossip moved on to the next story.

"In other news, villages on the outskirts of Ninjago are being terrorized by a gang of people known as Fire Fiends," she said.

The scene cut to an interview with one of the villagers, a terrified-looking man.

"These Fire Fiends—they worship a giant, flaming serpent!" the man said. "I've seen it with my own eyes!"

Kai's mouth dropped open.

"Fire Fang!" he cried. "Of course! Why didn't I think of it before?"

"Fire Fang?" Skylor asked. "You mean that enormous snake created by Aspheera?"

"Aspheera created Fire Fang after she stole *my* Elemental Powers," Kai reminded her. "Fire Fang's powers all come from me. All I have to do is find Fire Fang, and I can get my powers back!"

## Chapter Two
# The Fire Fiends

Kai raced for the door. Skylor pulled him back.

"Whoa, slow down, Kai," she said. "I mean, it's good to see you've got some pep back in your step, but are you seriously going to run to the outskirts of Ninjago wearing a stained sweatshirt in the middle of the night?"

Kai frowned. "Well . . . I hadn't exactly thought it out."

"I'll stay here and clean this up. You go home and get a good night's sleep," Skylor instructed. "Get your ninja gear out of the closet. I'll pick you up tomorrow with some supplies. This could be a dangerous journey."

"You don't need to come with me," Kai shot back. "This is a personal quest, and I've got to do it on my own. I can handle this. I can—"

*Plop!*

A flopping fish from the fish tank slid out of his sleeve and fell to the floor. Skylor gently picked it up and put it back in the tank with the others.

"I won't get in your way," she promised. "I know you've got this. It's just . . . maybe a road trip would be good for us. I mean, we haven't even been out on a real date yet."

"I visit you every night at the noodle shop," Kai protested.

"That does *not* count as a date," Skylor replied.

Kai couldn't argue. "All right. You can come with me."

*"Gee, thanks!"* Skylor replied, rolling her eyes. "See you at sunrise!"

Still dripping from his clash with the fish tank, Kai walked down the streets of Ninjago City to the small basement apartment he'd moved into after he lost his Fire Powers. He hadn't been the first to leave. Zane, the Ice Ninja, had retreated to the Samurai-X cave with the android P.I.X.A.L., who had created some experimental software that she thought would help Zane regain his Ice powers.

Then Cole, the Earth Ninja, had left the city for a simple life on a farm, and Jay—well, the Lightning Ninja didn't tell anyone where he was going. Nya, the Water Ninja, was busy saving the world in her revamped Samurai-X mech.

That had left Kai with Master Wu and Lloyd. When he wasn't busy helping to rebuild the monastery, the Green Ninja continued to train, and Lloyd had tried to get Kai to train with him every day. But Kai's heart just hadn't been in it.

"I want to try living an ordinary life," he'd said, and he'd packed a bag of clothes and ventured into Ninjago City. He found a place near the noodle shop, where he spent most of his free time. During the day he worked odd jobs around the city, and at five o'clock he headed to the restaurant and lingered there, talking to Skylor, eating noodles, and watching the giant TV.

There wasn't much to his apartment except a bed, a table, a bathroom, and a small kitchen area with a sink, mini fridge, and electric stovetop. The only time he spent there was to sleep. If he lingered for too long, he would be alone with his thoughts, and he hated that.

Kai changed out of his wet clothes and into some dry sweats. Then he pulled a duffel bag from under his bed and unzipped it. Inside, neatly folded, were his red ninja jacket, pants, and belt.

*I'm not sure if I'm ready for this,* Kai thought. *But tonight I let a bunch of inexperienced goons with a ridiculous name kick my butt, and Skylor had to save it. I need to be the Fire Ninja. And the only way I'm going to do that is to put on this uniform, defeat Fire Fang, and get my powers back!*

The next morning, Skylor pulled up in front of the building in a small, three-wheeled delivery vehicle with MR. CHEN'S NOODLE HOUSE in bright letters on the side.

"*This* is what we're driving on our adventure?" Kai asked, wearing his uniform.

"It's got all it takes for out-of-the-way deliveries," Skylor replied. "Don't be fussy. Hop in!"

Kai climbed into the passenger seat. Skylor grinned at him. "Looking good, Kai. Red is your

color," she said. "And your hair is styling."

"Thanks, uh . . . you look nice, too," Kai replied.

Skylor had donned her fighting uniform. Her hair was pulled back into a ponytail. She was an Elemental Master too, just like Kai had been. As the Master of Amber, she could temporarily use the powers of any other Elemental Master she touched. That meant that most of the time, she had to rely on her combat training in battle.

Skylor had inherited her Amber powers from her mother, and had been trained in the martial arts by her father. Master Chen had tried to take advantage of his daughter's power by luring all the Elemental Masters to an island so he could steal them—and that was how Skylor and Kai had met. Skylor had helped her dad at first, but decided in the end to help the ninja. She'd been an ally to them—and a good friend to Kai—ever since.

"So, where exactly are we going?" Kai asked as Skylor drove through the city streets.

"I called the NGTV station and got the coordinates for the village from the news story last night," Skylor replied. "It'll take us most of the day to get there. But I brought snacks!"

She held up a bag from the noodle shop. "Not-so-puffy potstickers. Not good enough for my customers, but just fine for a road trip."

They drove for hours, listening to music, snacking, and talking. Their journey took them out of the city, over rolling hills, and through farmland. By the afternoon, the terrain had changed to more open, flat land. Kai could see what looked like desert sands in the distance, bordered by low, reddish mountains.

"The village should be just over this ridge," Skylor said, and Kai looked at her with gratitude.

As much as he thought he needed to make this journey alone, it was good to have company, especially Skylor's. But he felt his palms sweat as they crossed the ridge.

*Can I really beat Fire Fang without my Elemental Powers?* he wondered to himself.

As they drove over the sprawling land, they soon spotted an oasis of green and activity nearby. A stream flowed down from one of the mountains and snaked through a small village. Modest homes and shops were clustered on either side of the stream, and crops grew on the western side of the settlement.

Skylor drove the delivery vehicle into the center of the village and parked. A curious crowd quickly approached.

"Noodle delivery? All the way out here?" a woman asked, as Skylor emerged from the vehicle.

"We're not selling food," Skylor replied. "We're here because—"

"IT'S KAI THE FAMOUS NINJA! HE'S COME TO SAVE US FROM THE FIRE FIENDS!" someone yelled, and the villagers began to swarm Kai.

"Okay, okay, everyone, please back off! You're messing up my hair," Kai said, and the villagers quieted down and obeyed as the ninja patted his hair back into place.

A cute little girl gazed at Kai with admiring eyes. "Is it true? Are you here to save us from the Fire Fiends?"

"Well, um, sure," Kai said. "I mean, we're looking for that big snake they hang around with, Fire Fang."

A man stepped forward and pointed north.

"You will find Fire Fang there, in the Lake of Fire," he said. "The snake came to the crater many months ago."

A white-haired woman chimed in. "Those who live around the crater have always worshipped fire. They kept to themselves. But when Fire Fang arrived, they worshipped him. And that's when the trouble started."

A teenage boy spoke up. "They began to attack the villages in this region, burning down houses and bringing the plunder back to Fire Fang."

"They have attacked us once already, and we're trying to rebuild," a man added.

Kai gazed around at the village, and saw what he hadn't noticed before. Some of the homes were just shells of charred wood. Other buildings were under construction with fireproof bricks made of red clay.

"How far away is this Lake of Fire?" he asked.

"Just an hour's journey in your truck," the man replied. "Although I must warn you, many have tried to face the Fire Fiends, and all have failed."

"But now we've got the Master of Fire on our side," the girl said, gazing at Kai with admiration.

"And the Master of Amber, too!" Skylor said

The man put a hand on his daughter's shoulder. "We're glad you're here, Kai, but haven't you . . . well, people say you've lost your powers."

"He's still a ninja!" Skylor interjected.

Kai frowned. "It's okay, Skylor. It's true. I don't have my Elemental Powers of Fire. But that's only temporary. As soon as I find Fire Fang—"

*Clang! Clang! Clang!*

A loud bell rang through the village.

"The Fire Fiends are attacking!" someone yelled, and before the villagers could flee, flaming balls of fire began to rain down!

"This way!" Skylor cried, and she raced toward the direction of the fireballs.

Kai followed her to the edge of the village, where a small army was lined up on the edge of the crop field. Each soldier wore a bright orange uniform with a protective vest, and a helmet shaped like a head of a snake. All the Fire Fiends held flaming torches, and several were operating red cannons shooting fire balls.

Kai's eyes narrowed. "Stand back, Skylor. I got this," he said. *"Ninjaaaaaaaa-go!"*

## Chapter Three
# The Lake of Fire

Kai spun into a Spinjitzu tornado and launched himself at the Fire Fiends. The soldiers in the first line thrust out their flaming torches as Kai approached. The ninja managed to knock down a few, but—

*"Ow! Ouch! Ow!"*

The flames singed Kai every time he made contact. He stopped spinning and rolled on the ground, putting out the flames.

Skylor raced up to him. "Kai, I have an idea. There's a—"

"I told you, I got this!" Kai cried, jumping to his feet. *"Ninjaaaaaaaaa— OW!"*

Kai tried to dodge the torches and fireballs, but there were too many Fire Fiends. Once again, he had to stop and put out the flames leaping from his uniform. Then—

*SPLASH!*

An enormous wave of water washed over Kai and the Fire Fiends, putting out the torches and disabling the fireball cannons. One of the Fire Fiends, who had golden flames attached to his helmet, cried out.

"Foul water! Hydration prevents our salvation!"

Kai shook the water out of his hair and turned to see Skylor, standing next to a toppled water tower in the field.

"I told you, I—" Kai began.

"Kai, Spinjitzu!" Skylor yelled.

*Of course!* Kai thought. *"Ninjaaaaaa-go!"*

He launched into another Spinjitzu tornado, and this time, it worked. One by one, he collided with the Fire Fiends, sending them flying.

"Retreat! Retreat!" cried their leader, and the Fire Fiends ran off.

Skylor approached Kai. "Now, that's what I call teamwork," she said with a grin.

"Yeah, well, thanks for your help, but I could have done it on my own," Kai muttered. He looked down and turned away from her.

*She knows I'm lying. Without my powers, I'm nothing,* he thought bitterly. *I need to find Fire Fang and get my powers back!*

Skylor frowned. "You know, Kai, I know you're going through something, so I'm being pretty patient with you. But I don't know how long that's going to last."

Kai sighed. "I'm sorry. I know you're trying to help. But I just know that if I don't do this on my own, it's not going to work!"

"How can you be so sure of that?" Skylor asked. "You of all people should know that working on a team is better than working alone. Where would you be without Master Wu and the other ninja?"

"I don't know. Maybe I'd still have my powers," Kai grumbled.

Skylor shook her head. "This is not the Kai I know," she said.

"I'm not the Kai *I* know," he replied.

"Fine," Skylor said. "Let's get you to Fire Fang and see if your plan works. Let's jump in our three-wheeler, and—"

"Maybe you should stay here, and protect the village," Kai said.

Skylor shook her head. "Those hotheads retreated as soon as they got a little wet. I don't think they'll be back anytime soon. This is the perfect time to get to Fire Fang."

"All right," Kai reluctantly agreed. *But don't get in my way,* he thought.

They made their way back to the delivery vehicle and got directions to the Lake of Fire from the villagers. Kai and Skylor made the hour trip in silence.

Skylor slowed down when the crater came into view, and pulled behind a rock formation. "We should probably walk the rest of the way, so the Fire Fiends don't see us coming," she suggested.

"Sounds good," Kai agreed, and they exited the vehicle.

The Lake of Fire was a huge circle of flames at the base of one of the mountains. Jagged red rocks surrounded the lake's perimeter. There was

no sign of the Fire Fiends—or Fire Fang—except for a giant, stone statue of Fire Fang, overlooking one side of the fiery lake.

"This *must* be the place," Skylor quipped.

"How can a Lake of Fire exist, anyway?" Kai wondered out loud. "Is it some kind of magic?"

"It looks like a crater to me," Skylor replied. "There must be natural gas escaping from fissures in the crater. And all it would take is one spark—"

"And the crater would burn, and keep burning until the natural gas runs out," Kai realized. "That's pretty cool, actually."

"*Hot* is more like it," Skylor said, breaking into a grin. "I'm starting to sweat. Let's take a quick break and come up with a plan."

She ducked behind another large rock and Kai followed. Skylor peered out from behind it.

"It looks deserted," she said. "But see, on the opposite side of the crater? That looks like an entrance into the mountain. Maybe that's where they all live."

Kai spied the cavelike entrance and his eyes lit up. "Fire Fang's *got* to be in there! Time to get my powers back!"

He darted out from behind the rock and raced toward the crater.

"Kai, no, wait!" Skylor cried out.

*I'm not going to let her stop me from doing what I have to,* Kai thought, and he launched into Spinjitzu and whirled across the sand toward the Lake of Fire.

Seconds later, he came to a stop. The heat from the crater assaulted him, but he didn't turn back. He climbed to the rim of the crater, where a pathway around the perimeter led to the mountain entrance.

*Fire Fang's gotta be in there!* Kai thought, and he sprinted along the edge of the fiery crater . . .

. . . until the surface beneath his feet dropped, and he plummeted toward the leaping flames below!

## Chapter Four
# Fire Fang

Kai felt a hand grab his wrist and pull him up. Skylor had saved him!

"Oh, boy! You're tough to keep up with," Skylor said, panting.

"What—I don't understand. I didn't slip, did I?" Kai asked.

Skylor shook her head. "Nope. I think it was a booby trap," she said. "You must have stepped on a stone that gave way under your weight."

She motioned to a square-shaped hole in the pathway that she had just pulled him from.

*She's right*, he thought. But instead of gratitude, confusion and anger bubbled up inside him.

"You didn't have to try to catch up to me!" he yelled. "You don't even need to be here."

"Oh, no? I just saved you from an extra-crispy fate!" Skylor shot back.

"Just stop saving me, okay? I'll never get my powers back if I don't do this myself," Kai replied. "I don't need you, Skylor!"

The glare in her eyes faded and was replaced by a flicker of hurt.

"Sure, Kai," Skylor said. "Good luck trying to defeat Fire Fang on your own."

She hopped over the hole in the path and jogged back to the delivery vehicle.

Kai felt a quick pang of regret as he watched her go, and then brushed it aside.

*Skylor's the best,* he thought. *But this is my quest, not hers. I need to do this alone.*

Remembering her warning about booby traps, Kai slowly made his way to the cave entrance, jumping over any cracks he saw in the path. When he reached the cave entrance, he paused.

"Looks too easy," he said, and as a precaution, he picked up a rock and threw it through the opening.

*Whoosh!* Flames shot up from the bottom of the entrance way. If Kai had walked through it, he would have been toast!

The flames receded, and Kai frowned. *There has to be a way to beat this,* he thought. He tossed another rock.

*Whoosh!* The flames leapt up again, and then started to recede.

*Gotta get the timing just right,* Kai thought, and he tossed a third rock through the opening.

*Here goes nothing,* and he jumped over the flames just as they died down, spinning into a somersault when he hit the ground.

The flames leapt up behind him—but he had safely avoided them. Kai grinned.

"See, Skylor? I don't need help," he announced into the darkness of the cave.

In the distance, Kai heard what sounded like rhythmic chanting. He moved forward slowly and carefully, traveling through a cramped tunnel-like passageway through the mountain.

The path opened up into a large, bowl-shaped room. Fire Fiends in their orange armor marched in a circle around a serpent half as tall as a Ninjago City skyscraper. Black scales rippled down the creature's body, yellow eyes glowed inside his face, and two long, sharp fangs grew from its wide mouth. Horns grew from the serpent's head, and a cobra's hood fanned out from behind them. The fire inside the creature burned hot, glowing orange-red between his scales and flickering throughout his hood.

*Fire Fang!* Kai thought. *And that's* my *fire running through those veins!*

Kai heard the chant of the Fire Fiends more clearly now.

"We hail you, Fire Fang! We are your loyal gang!"

*They're not carrying their torches,* Kai thought. *So I should be able to get past them. But then what? Aspheera used sorcery to steal my Fire powers when she gave them to Fire Fang. But I'm no magician.*

The ninja stared at Fire Fang, thinking. He felt especially drawn to the snake's yellow eyes . . . but forced himself to look away.

*They're hypnotic,* Kai thought as an idea came to him. *I need to distract him, and then get close enough to steal my power back. . . .*

Kai stepped out of the dark tunnel.

*"Ninjaaaaaaaaaaa-go!"* he cried.

"Intruder!" yelled the leader of the Fire Fiends, and they all scrambled to light their torches.

Fire Fang hissed and shot a blast of fire at Kai. Spinning, he narrowly avoided it. Then he launched himself into the air.

Still spinning, Kai soared up, up, up to the Fire Fang's eyes. He twirled back and forth, back and forth, and the giant beast began to sway. The fiery glow beneath his scales and hood subsided.

The hypnotic spin of Kai's Spinjitzu tornado had both confused and calmed the creature.

Seeing his chance, Kai stopped spinning and leapt onto the back of Fire Fang's head. He wasn't sure what he was supposed to do, but he knew he had to try. He placed both hands on Fire Fang's hot scales.

"Okay, Fire Fang, give it back to me! Give me back my fire!"

Fire Fang stirred, and Kai heard the creature hiss. The serpent's scales became hotter to touch, and

Kai could spot the fiery glow growing under them.

"Come on, it's mine! GIVE ME MY FIRE BACK!" Kai yelled.

Fire Fang roared and thrashed his head, sending Kai tumbling to the ground. He landed on a pile of rocky rubble mixed with plundered treasures that the Fire Fiends had collected for Fire Fang—mostly metal tools and pots and pans, and other items that wouldn't burn. Fire Fang aimed a fiery blast at him, and Kai rolled out of the way.

Kai tried to rise to his feet, but Fire Fang's thrashed wildly, sending heavy rocks tumbling onto Kai's legs, pinning him in place. Fire Fang leaned over Kai, who looked into those yellow eyes once again.

*This fire—this fire has nothing to do with me,* he thought. *It's not mine anymore. It's Fire Fang's. I can't take it. I need to find it within myself somehow.*

Then he saw another fire blast forming, deep inside the creature's throat. . . .

## Chapter Five
# Fighting Fire with Fire

"Nice try, Toothy!"

Skylor raced into the cave and flipped into the offerings pile, picking up a large, metal garbage can lid as her feet landed. Then she jumped between Kai and Fire Fang and blocked the fiery blast, using the lid as a shield.

Kai quickly kicked away from the rocks and jumped to his feet. Skylor dropped the red-hot shield and Kai saw she was wearing Master Chen's fireproof oven mitts on her hands.

*Why didn't I think of those?* he thought.

They ran away just as— *Whoosh!* Fire Fang aimed another blast of fire at them. They ran into the tunnel, speeding toward the Lake of Fire.

Kai stopped and looked at Skylor.

"You didn't leave after all," he said.

Skylor shrugged. "Like I said, you're not yourself. I thought maybe I should keep an eye on you. And it's a good thing I did."

Kai flashed back to the smell of Fire Fang's hot breath, and the feeling of helplessness as the creature pinned him down. Without Skylor, he'd be toast!

He remembered the time he had discovered his True Potential, when he realized he needed to protect the Green Ninja. Everything he did from then on, every decision he made, was based on protecting others.

Then he thought about what Skylor had tried to tell him—about all the other times his sister, Nya, and his friends, Lloyd, Cole, Jay and Zane, had helped him in a tight spot. They'd saved him, and he'd saved them, and together they'd been able to save countless others.

"I can't protect others unless I let other people protect me, too," he realized out loud.

As he said the words, his eyes glowed red and he felt the power flow within him. Fire sprouted from his hands.

"Kai!" Skylor cried. "Your fire powers are back!"

"Yes," he said. "And just in time."

The cry of the Fire Fiends echoed from the tunnel as they charged toward the Lake of Fire.

"Hey, Skylor," Kai said, looking her directly in the eyes.

"What?" Skylor asked.

"Power up," he said. "We're finishing this together. You were right all along. I can't defeat Fire Fang and the Fire Fiends without your help!"

Skylor touched his arm, and an orange glow swept through her body and then faded. Red flame flashed in her eyes.

"Ready," she said. "Time to fight fire with fire!"

*"Aaaaaaaaaaaaaaaaaaaaaaaah!"*

The Fire Fiends charged out of the cave entrance, holding their flaming torches.

*Whoosh!* Kai and Skylor shot fireballs at the attackers. The flames hit their fireproof armor and harmlessly fanned out. Kai and Skylor kept shooting fireballs, and the Fire Fiends continued to advance.

Kai frowned—and then he had a thought.

"They can carry fire, but we can manipulate it!" he called out.

Skylor grinned. "Right!"

Kai pointed at the flaming torch of one of the Fire Fiends. He raised his hand and the flame lifted up from the torch and floated in the air. Then Kai swung his arm behind him, and the flame flew through the air and joined the flames in the Lake of Fire.

"Nice!" Skylor cheered. "But can you do a double?" She held out both arms. Concentrating, she manipulated the flames on two more torches. Fire Fiends charged at her, and she held out both arms again. But the fiends kept coming, their torches bright with flame.

"My power ran out!" she cried.

"I got this," Kai said. "After all, you've saved me a bunch of times already. Now I can return the favor. *Ninjaaaaaa-go!*"

Kai spun into a Spinjitzu tornado, knocking the Fire Fiends off the rim of the crater. Skylor changed tactics and kicked the torches out of their hands so Kai could easily finish them. When the last fiend was toppled, Kai whirled over to Skylor for a high five.

"I think we qualify as a power couple now," he said, and then . . .

*WHOOOOOSH!*

A huge wave of fire blasted from inside the tunnel. Kai and Skylor dove in opposite directions to escape it.

Fire Fang emerged into the daylight. Flames leapt from the serpent's hood. Kai looked at Skylor.

"I got this! I mean it this time," he said.

Skylor grinned. "Glad to see the old Kai is back!"

Kai turned back to Fire Fang.

"Did you think we forgot about you, pal?" he called out. "Your little goons can't protect you now!" Kai's eyes glowed as he built up the power inside him for a massive blast. He extended both arms toward Fire Fang.

*WHOMP!* The fiery assault hit the serpent straight on. Fire Fang wobbled, but when the smoke cleared, the fireproof scales had largely protected the creature. Fire Fang's mouth opened . . .

"Nice try," Kai said, and he raised his arms and concentrated as the ferocious blast shot out. The flame flew up, over the creature's head, and crashed into the mountain, where it fizzled against the rocks.

"Skylor, I need your help!" Kai called out.

"You got it!" Skylor replied.

*Whirrrrrrrrrrrr!* Kai rocketed toward Fire Fang in a Spinjitzu tornado. Skylor raced across the crater to join him.

*BAM!* Kai and Skylor made contact, sending the creature flying off the crater. Stunned, the giant serpent lay motionless on the sand.

"He won't be down for long," Kai remarked.

"Yeah," Skylor agreed. "We need to find some way to protect the villages from—"

*Vroooooooom!* The sound of a small army of motors interrupted her. Kai and Skylor spun around to see dozens of trucks and cars making their way toward the Lake of Fire. They ran to greet them.

The man they recognized from the village got out of an all-terrain vehicle.

"We all talked, and we thought it wasn't fair for you both to face Fire Fang and the Fire Fiends alone," he said. "Do you need any help?"

Kai and Skylor looked at each other and grinned.

"What do you think?" Skylor asked. "I mean, we need help, but what can the villagers do?"

Kai glanced over at the giant statue of Fire Fang. "Hmm. I think there's something we can all do together."

A short time later, Kai stood on top of the Fire Fang statue. Dozens of ropes had been tied around it. The ropes were stretched across the lake and secured to the bumpers of all the villagers' vehicles.

"Let's do this!" Kai yelled, and the engines roared as they surged forward. Kai jumped down off the statue's head as—*WHOMP!* The statue fell head-first into the Lake of Fire, smothering the flames in the crater!

The Fire Fiends, groggy from their Spinjitzu schooling, stumbled toward the crater. Smoke from the smothered fire wafted up from the edges.

"Our fire!" they moaned.

The villagers cheered. Kai and Skylor high-fived. Then Skylor frowned.

"Wait, Fire Fang must be recovered by now," she said.

Kai and Skylor raced back to the spot of the crater where Fire Fang had fallen. The creature was gone.

"Whoa! It just vanished," Skylor remarked.

"Maybe looking for a new place to hang out," Kai guessed.

"Aspheera created Fire Fang," Skylor pointed out. "Maybe it returned back to elemental energy."

"We may never know," Kai added.

They made their way back to the cheering villagers.

"So, you've got your powers back," Skylor said. "What now?"

"Well, I guess I'll go back to Master Wu and Lloyd, and see if there's any news from the other ninja," Kai said. "They might need my . . . I mean, *our* help."

Skylor nodded.

"But first, you and I need to celebrate!" Kai added.

"What do you have in mind?" Skylor asked.

"I was thinking," Kai said as he hopped into the passenger seat of the noodle delivery vehicle, "maybe it's time to find out what this new red-hot team of Kai and Skylor can do together? I mean, the city is a real mess right now."

Skylor grinned. "I'm in," she said, starting the engine. "No sleep till Ninjago City!"

# Chapter One
# Looking for Clues

"Zane, please hold still," P.I.X.A.L. said in a patient voice.

"I am holding still," Zane protested.

"No, you are not," P.I.X.A.L. countered. "Now, I just have one more sensor to attach to your circuits . . ."

P.I.X.A.L. and Zane were busy in the Samurai-X cave, located deep beneath the Sea of Sand. They had retreated to Nya's old hideout after their underground hangar bay became buried in the rubble of the Monastery of Spinjitzu during the

assault of the Crystal King. Filled with computers, vehicles, and parts to build mechs, PIXAL had found the alternate space to be very useful. In the weeks since the ninja had lost their Elemental Powers, the android had dedicated herself to finding a way to help Zane restore his power of Ice.

Zane's journey to become the Titanium Ninja contained many twists and turns. This extraordinary Nindroid was created by the brilliant Dr. Julien and then given the power of Ice from the Elemental Ice Master. Yet, before he passed away, Dr. Julien, had turned off Zane's memory switch. Believing he was just an ordinary boy, Master Wu took in the Nindroid and trained him to be a ninja along with Kai, Cole, and Jay.

Zane regained the memory of who he was, but as the ninja faced ever-growing challenges, his memories came and went. He was nearly destroyed during a battle with the Overlord, and then reborn again as the Titanium Ninja. PIXAL helped him regain his memories then.

Later, when Zane had used the Scroll of Forbidden Spinjitzu to try to stop Aspheera, he became stranded in the Never-Realm. The evil General Vex had found him and erased his memories, manipulating him so that he became the cruel Ice Emperor. Then Lloyd had helped Zane remember his true identity. And recently, when the Crystal King set his forces on Ninjago, Zane had crashed his mech and damaged his memory circuit. He reverted back to his Ice Emperor programming, and this time, it took the brilliant engineer Cyrus Borg to repair him.

P.I.X.A.L. believed that the key to Zane's recovering his power of Ice was connected to exploring these fractured memories.

"We must look for clues," she had said. "And I believe those clues can be found within you."

Zane had complete trust in his android friend, because P.I.X.A.L. understood him better than anyone else. But the idea of exploring his memories made him uneasy. Some lost memories felt like an ache deep inside him. And he would rather not think about some of the things he could remember.

He twitched nervously in his chair as P.I.X.A.L. inserted a sensor into a port in the back of his head.

"These sensors are critical to your journey," she explained, in her calm, steady voice. "They will immerse you in your memories so you can experience them as though you are actually there."

Zane twitched again. "And will others in the memory be able to see or hear me?"

"No," P.I.X.A.L. replied. "You will be an observer only. Now keep still."

She stepped away from him and moved to the large bank of computer screens. They cast a blue glow on her silver hair and the purple conduit lines on her face.

"It will be interesting to see if this technology can restore your Elemental Powers," she remarked as she entered a code into the system. "I am working on a way to adapt the tech to work with biological memory banks, perhaps helping the other ninja regain their powers."

"I am sure they are all searching for a way to unlock their True Potential again," Zane replied. "Although it is rather odd that I have not heard from any of them."

P.I.X.A.L. spun around in her chair and fixed her green eyes on Zane.

"For this first session, I will bring you out of the program in four minutes and thirty seconds," she said. "If something goes wrong, or you want to leave the memory, just say something."

*If something goes wrong . . .* , he thought. An image of the Ice Emperor's face, cold and fierce, flashed through his mind.

"Understood," Zane replied.

"Are you ready?" P.I.X.A.L. asked.

"Ready."

P.I.X.A.L. turned back to the computer. "Initiating memory exploration in three . . . two . . . one!"

## Chapter Two
# The Face of Fear

Zane felt like he was falling . . . and falling . . . and falling. Then his feet suddenly touched the ground. His sensors immediately detected a change in temperature. It was freezing.

*Is this an Ice Emperor memory?* he wondered, and his fear circuits quickened.

*Rowwwwwwwwwr!*

The memory appeared in front of his eyes. An enormous blue Ice Dragon thrashed its head. Its body glowed with frostlike energy waves. Bright white lights glowed behind its narrow eyes. Sharp teeth that looked like silver icicles gnashed in the creature's mouth.

The Ice Dragon was in a large, dark cave. Cowering against the wall, he saw himself, right after he had become the Titanium Ninja. He wore a simple white uniform, and his face and arms gleamed with the brightness of the new, superstrong metal that formed his body.

*I look so afraid,* Zane thought. *The details of how I transformed from the White Ninja to the Titanium Ninja are very sketchy. My memory banks were damaged when it happened. But I do remember this: Master Chen imprisoned me in this cave. I experienced strange, terrifying visions and dreams. I did not accept that I had become the Titanium Ninja.*

Inside this memory, he watched himself struggle with fear and doubt.

"I am not the White Ninja. I am just a replica," Memory Zane said. "I'm . . . afraid. My powers can't stop him!"

Memory Zane cowered as the dragon roared again.

Watching the memory unfold before him, Zane remembered that P.I.X.A.L. had communicated with him through this whole event.

"Close your eyes," P.I.X.A.L. had said. "Close your eyes and see there is nothing to fear."

Memory Zane closed his eyes.

"I am not the White Ninja. I am not the White Ninja," he said.

"Who are you, then?" P.I.X.A.L. had asked.

Memory Zane stood up. He gazed down at his shining metal body. And then his eyes flashed. He understood.

"I am . . . the Titanium Ninja," he said slowly. Then he raised his voice. "I am the Titanium Ninja!"

Memory Zane went to the dragon, smiled, and placed a hand on the creature's neck.

Then the image of the memory blurred and cackled with static. Zane felt like he was falling again. The scene became clear, and he found himself in a new memory. He was standing in front of Master Chen's palace, looking out over the island. The ninja and the Elemental Masters stared at the sky as Master Chen and his goons took off in jets, stranding everyone there.

"I'll go alone," Lloyd was saying.

"And take on his whole army?" Nya asked.

Lloyd threw up his arms. "I'm the only one of us who can summon an elemental dragon."

"Not anymore!"

Zane looked up. The Ice Dragon swooped down from the sky, ridden by Memory Zane. The ninja and the Elemental Masters cheered.

"Zane, you gotta tell us how you did that!" Jay said.

"I faced my fear," Memory Zane replied. "I realized that it wasn't something in front of me holding me back. It was something inside me!"

Zane watched as the memory ended happily as Kai, Cole, and Jay all created their elemental dragons, too.

*To truly become the Titanium Ninja, I had to overcome my fears,* Zane realized. *Is fear what is holding me back now?*

Zane tried to think about what he might be afraid of. Then a thought echoed in his circuits.

*I am just a replica.*

That's what Memory Zane had said before. But what did he mean?

*I have been many things,* Zane thought. *I have been the son of Dr. Julien. I have been the White Ninja. The Titanium Ninja. The Ice Ninja. The Ice Emperor.*

*I have been all of those things. But who am I, really?*

Then the memory went black.

## Chapter Three
# Back to the Beginning

Zane's eyes fluttered. He was back in the cave underneath the monastery. P.I.X.A.L.'s green eyes were staring at him.

"I monitored your systems while you were exploring your memories," she said. "There was a marked fluctuation in your stress levels. Were you able to figure out how to recover your Elemental Powers?"

"Negative," Zane said. "However, the experience was helpful. In the past, I learned that I needed to face my fears. But I do not believe that is what I need to do now."

"Would you like to try again?" P.I.X.A.L. asked.

"I would like to try something different," Zane replied, rising from his chair. "Your program was very successful in implanting me inside a memory. I remembered learning how to manifest my Ice Dragon. Perhaps, to connect with my power of Ice, I must return to ice. I would like to return to the Frozen Lake."

"I hope you succeed," P.I.X.A.L. replied.

"Thank you, P.I.X.A.L.," Zane said.

He climbed onto one of the cycles in the hangar bay and sped through the tunnel leading out of the Samurai-X cave. As he sped through the winding roads of Ninjago, his mind drifted back to P.I.X.A.L.'s experiment.

*I am not afraid of anything—or am I?* he thought. *Perhaps meditation can reveal what my memories could not.*

He finally stopped in front of a lake capped with a thin layer of ice—the Frozen Lake. He smiled. As a young man, before he knew he was a Nindroid, he had impressed people with his ability to hold his breath underwater. That was where Master Wu had found him and invited him to become a ninja—meditating at the bottom of the lake.

Zane climbed off the cycle and dove through the ice. He swam down, down into the freezing water, his circuits protected by his titanium frame. When he reached the bottom, he sat cross-legged and closed his eyes.

At first, he just enjoyed the ice-cold water as it hit his temperature sensors. His childhood memories were sketchy, but he did remember that cold always made him feel calm.

His mind began to drift. . . . *What is Cole doing right now? Do I have enough fuel to get back to the monastery? Why does Master Wu love tea so much?* Then he tried to bring his thoughts back to his purpose.

*What is it I need to learn to recover my Elemental Powers?*

He tried to clear his mind of all thoughts and concentrate on the feeling of being cold. Cold like the ice skimming the top of the lake. Cold like the wind coming down from the mountains. Cold like the ground after a fresh snow . . .

Suddenly, the ice water began to spin and whirl, and once again Zane felt like he was falling. The scene around him changed, and instead of the bottom of the lake, he found himself in a snowy forest, surrounded by tall birch trees.

"Birchwood Forest," Zane said. "But how—how did I get here?"

Then he heard P.I.X.A.L.'s concerned voice inside his head.

"Zane, something has happened to launch the memory program remotely," she informed him. "The memory sensors have all been activated. I have a theory that your meditative state might have triggered it somehow. Would you like me to end the program?"

Zane gazed around the forest. "No," he replied. "If my meditation brought me here, then perhaps this is a memory I must experience."

He walked down the path, hearing the snow crunch underneath his feet. He stopped at a very large birch tree with a round door carved into the trunk. He opened the door and stepped inside Dr. Julien's hidden workshop. It was a simple space, with a creaky wood floor, a potbellied stove to keep his father warm, and a large worktable. Dr. Julien's tools hung from hooks on the walls.

The workshop had been his home for years. And now here he was, reliving a memory that his father had tried to bury.

There on the cot lay Dr. Julien, old and taking his last breaths. Zane's younger self, in a body that looked more human than Nindroid, held his father's hand.

"You were always the son I never had," Dr. Julien said in a weak voice. "It's time you begin your next stage in life. And the only reason I'm about to do this is because . . . I love you."

Dr. Julien took off his eyeglasses and smiled at Memory Zane, who smiled back. A tear fell down Zane's cheek as he watched the memory unfold before his eyes.

Dr. Julien opened Memory Zane's control panel.

Zane knew what was about to happen. "No! Don't do it!" he yelled.

But Dr. Julien could not hear him. He shut down the young Nindroid's memory banks. A blank look came across Memory Zane's face. With no memory of his father, or his past, he walked out of the workshop and into the snow.

Complicated feelings bubbled up in Zane as he watched his younger self leave. The first time he had relived that memory was when he, Cole, Jay, and Kai had traveled to the Birchwood Forest together. Zane had discovered his memory switch and learned the truth about his past.

He now remembered that he had been built to protect those who cannot protect themselves. His father had empowered him to unlock his True Potential by recognizing the obstacles holding him back. That allowed him to tap into all of his Elemental Powers to become the strongest ninja he could be. Unlocking True Potential was a goal of every Elemental Master, and that moment in his past had filled him with confidence.

But now he felt defeated.

*What would have happened if Dr. Julien had not turned off my memory switch?* he wondered. *Would my life have turned out differently?*

## Chapter Four
# An Icy History

Zane waited for the memory in Dr. Julien's workshop to end, but nothing happened. Curious, he left the hideout. He spotted the footprints of his younger self in the snow and followed them.

The blank expression on the young Nindroid's face was gone, replaced by one of peace. The boy was happily building a snowman.

*I don't remember this at all,* Zane thought. In fact, I have never explored the memories of the time between when Dr. Julien erased my memories, and Master Wu asked me to train with him.

The scene in front of him swirled, and Zane felt himself falling into a new memory. This time, young Memory Zane was sitting on a rock next to a frozen pond, affixing a blade to a pair of ice skates that looked handmade. He slipped the skates on his feet and then glided onto the ice, gracefully circling the pond as though he had been skating for years.

Then the scene blurred and Zane fell through space as the memory changed again. Zane was still in Birchwood Forest, standing in front of a small house made of blocks of ice. He approached and looked through the window. There, on a bed made of ice blocks, his young self was sleeping peacefully. Zane smiled.

"I was alone back then, but I appear to be happy," Zane said out loud. Then the scene began to swirl. . . .

"Help! Help!"

In this new memory, Zane watched as a father and daughter ran across the snow, pursued by a Treehorn! The dangerous creatures were the worst thing about Birchwood Forest. They looked almost like giant, lanky, four-legged spiders with long necks, droopy heads, and sharp tails. Black markings dotted their pale blue skin, and red eyes stared blankly from their faces. They were creepy, fast, and hungry.

"Help!" the father cried. The Treehorn was catching up on them quickly.

Zane charged toward the Treehorn, crying, *"Ninjaaaaa-go!"*

He tried to slam into the creature with a Spinjitzu tornado, but instead passed right through it. He'd totally forgotten he was just an observer to the memory.

*What is this?* he thought. *Am I to watch this poor family be attacked?*

"Hey, Treehorn! You can't catch me!" shouted a familiar voice.

Memory Zane, still young, sped down a snowy hill, riding a handmade snowboard. He zipped

past the Treehorn. The creature's head snapped in Memory Zane's direction, and it gave chase.

*"Wheeeeeeeeee!"* Memory Zane cried as he expertly led the Treehorn on a chase up and down the snowy hills.

Zane ran after them, curious to see what would happen.

*He is . . . I mean, I was fearless,* Zane thought.

Memory Zane slid down another hill on his snowboard—and sped toward a cliff! Zane gasped. What was his younger self thinking? Then . . .

Memory Zane did a backflip on his snowboard right at the edge of the cliff. He landed safely a few yards back—and the giant Treehorn tumbled over the edge!

"Yes!" Memory Zane cheered.

He made sure the beast was not coming back, then he tucked the snowboard under his arm and ran back to check on the father and daughter.

"Thank you so much, young man," the father said. "You saved us from that Treehorn."

"Well, happy to offer my assistance," Memory Zane replied.

Zane watched his younger self, stunned.

*This boy has no memory of his past,* he thought. *But he loves the cold and the ice. He protects those who need protection. Even without my memories, I was still Zane.*

The scene began to swirl again, and Zane felt a pang of sadness as he watched his smiling younger self disappear. Then he tensed. What new memory would he be visiting now?

The scene came together before his eyes. A throne room in a sinister palace made of cold, gray stone. A tall stone staircase led to a platform holding the throne. Seated in it was a man with armor, with ice-cold gleaming eyes, a hideous mask over his mouth, and holding a staff covered with ice crystals that glowed with the power of the Scroll of Forbidden Spinjitzu. The Ice Emperor.

"P.I.X.A.L., get me out of this memory!" Zane yelled.

## Chapter Five
# Forgiveness

The static sounded like a buzzing of a thousand bees as P.I.X.A.L. pulled Zane from the memory and the Ice Emperor's throne room disappeared. Zane's body lurched as he found himself back at the bottom of the Frozen Lake. He quickly swam up and broke through the ice. Then he hurried to the ninja cave.

"Welcome back, Zane," P.I.X.A.L. said. "I am quite surprised that the memory program launched remotely. The activation module's sensory circuit has showed no errors. I will have to double-check the sub-beta algorithms again. I am glad, however, that we were still able to communicate. Tell me, what happened in that last memory that made you want to leave?"

"I must confess something," Zane began. "I am reluctant to face myself as the Ice Emperor."

"The Ice Emperor can't hurt you inside a memory," she reminded him.

"No, that is not it," he said. "I am not worried that the Ice Emperor will hurt me. It's difficult to describe, but I think it has something to do with the terrible things I did when *I* was the Ice Emperor. That is not something I allow myself to think about often."

P.I.X.A.L.'s eyes flashed with sympathy. "Oh, Zane."

"The Ice Emperor was cruel and merciless," Zane said. "I would never do any of the things he did. How could the Ice Emperor be so unlike me? I should have been able to stop myself. How can I ever forgive myself?"

"I know that what happened to you in the Never-Realm was not your fault," P.I.X.A.L. told him. "But I also know that you must figure this out on your own."

Zane gazed over at the computer screen. "I . . . I cannot. I am too afraid."

"You have faced your fears before, Zane," P.I.X.A.L. reminded him. "And I believe that is what you must do now."

Zane nodded and slowly sat back in the chair. P.I.X.A.L. returned to the computer.

"I should be able to send you directly to a memory in the Never-Realm," she said. "Are you ready? Initiating memory exploration in three . . . two . . . one . . ."

Zane felt himself falling again. Suddenly, he was back in the throne room of the Ice Emperor. A menacing figure entered the room next to him. Cold eyes glared beneath his gray, armored helmet. Blue ice crystals clung to his long mustache, and an armored vest clanked as he moved. He stopped at the bottom of the stairs.

*General Vex!* Zane remembered

"My Emperor," General Vex said.

"How dare you disturb my thoughts," the Ice Emperor growled.

"I bring a warning, my Emperor," Vex said. "Strangers from a distant realm come to challenge you. They may be here for the prisoner—and to defy your rule."

Zane heard the crackling of ice as the Ice Emperor rose from his throne.

"They must be punished," the Ice Emperor ordered.

General Vex leaned in. "They must be destroyed. Show them your might. Show them what happens to those who defy the Emperor."

"Send my Blizzard Samurai," the Ice Emperor said. "Command them to destroy the strangers."

"And all who aid them," Vex added.

"And all who aid them," the Ice Emperor repeated.

Vex chuckled and left the throne room. The Ice Emperor sat back down.

Rage filled Zane. He marched up the stairs to the throne.

"Why do you listen to him!" Zane yelled. "These are lives you are destroying! Innocent lives! HOW CAN YOU DO THIS?"

The Ice Emperor's eyes flashed. "Who dares to disturb my thoughts now?"

"It's me, Z— Wait, you can hear me?" Zane asked.

"Intruder!" the Ice Emperor yelled, and he stood up once more. He pointed his staff right at Zane.

*He can see and hear me!* Zane thought. *How is this even possible?*

The Ice Emperor shot a powerful beam of white light at Zane. Zane jumped off the staircase and the beam left a string of sharp ice chards where he had just been standing.

Zane heard P.I.X.A.L.'s voice in his head.

"Zane, there is some kind of glitch happening," she said, and her voice sounded worried. "You have left your memory banks and it appears that you have entered your subconscious circuits. Because these are your thoughts, you can interact with them. Do you want me to try to extract you?"

"No, P.I.X.A.L.!" Zane replied. "I must see this through."

"You cannot escape me!" the Ice Emperor growled, and he shot another powerful blast from his staff. Zane rolled out of the way.

*I must get the staff away from him,* Zane thought. *Then maybe I can talk to him. I can figure out how he is able to do such terrible things.*

"*Ninjaaaaa-go!*" Zane whirled toward the Ice Emperor, dodging another icy blast from the staff. But before he could make contact with the Ice

Emperor, he waved the staff in a circle around him and put up an icy wall of defense.

"Are you afraid of *me*, then?" Zane asked.

"I fear nothing!" the Ice Emperor growled, and the ice wall around him shattered. He pointed the staff at Zane, who tried to jump out of the way. But the ice from the blast surrounded his legs, pinning him to the ground.

The Ice Emperor stomped toward him. "I will finish you now."

"Why?" Zane asked. "Why are you so cruel? How could you let this happen to you? Why weren't you strong enough to resist?"

The Ice Emperor paused, and his cold eyes flashed. "I was reprogrammed," he answered.

*Bzzzzzzzzzzzzzt!* Static crackled, the memory blurred, and Zane felt himself falling. He saw his younger self next to his crashed mech.

P.I.X.A.L.'s voice crackled in his head. "Zane, you have returned to your memory circuits. But the glitch could return at any time."

Zane watched as Vex tiptoed up behind Memory Zane, who was plugged into his mech's system, trying to fix it. Suddenly, Memory Zane's eyes went blank as Vex sneakily pulled out the plug.

"Rebooting," the computer voice intoned. "All systems online. Memory cache empty."

Vex gave an evil chuckle as the lights came back on in the Nindroid's eyes.

"Who are you?" Memory Zane asked.

"I am Vex, your . . . loyal advisor."

"And who am *I*?" the Nindroid asked.

Zane watched and listened to the memory. Vex told Memory Zane lie after lie. He convinced

Memory Zane that he was the Ice Emperor whose throne had been stolen from him. Then he handed the Nindroid the staff powered by the Scroll of Forbidden Spinjitzu, and the staff's evil energy coursed through Memory Zane's body.

"Nooooooo!" Zane cried out.

*Bzzzzzzzzzt!* The memory disappeared, and Zane fell into a new one.

The scene disappeared, and Zane entered a new memory. The Ice Emperor sat on his throne, but he was not yet old and covered in stone armor. His body coursed with the blue energy of the Scroll of Forbidden Spinjitzu.

General Vex approached the throne. "My Emperor, there is a village in your kingdom that refuses to honor you with an offering of fish. We must teach them a lesson and destroy their village."

The Ice Emperor's eyes flickered. "Destroy a village? Over fish?"

*He's trying to resist!* Zane thought, as he watched the memory unfold.

"They defy you, my lord," Vex said. "It will begin with fish, and end with your doom! Do you want that?"

The power of Forbidden Spinjitzu flared from the top of the Emperor's head, responding to Vex's words.

"Destroy the village, then," the Ice Emperor said calmly.

"No!" Zane yelled, but the Ice Emperor could not hear him. "This is not you! You protect others! You do not harm them!"

*Bzzzzzzzzzzzzt!* Static erased the scene, and Zane lurched into a new memory, one familiar to him. The Ice Emperor was about to finish off Lloyd at Vex's urging. But seeing Lloyd, hearing his true name—Zane—and listening to Vex use the word "protect" triggered something deep inside him.

"Protect those . . . who cannot protect themselves," the Ice Emperor said. Those words restored all the memories that had been erased, and at the same time the spell was broken. The Ice Emperor transformed back into Zane and cast off the Scroll of Forbidden Spinjitzu.

Zane watched the memory unfold before him, amazed.

*I was fighting Vex the whole time,* Zane thought. *Even with my memory wiped! But the power of the Scroll of Forbidden Spinjitzu was just too strong. Evil was imposed on me. Even when I was not Zane, I was still Zane. It was not my fault.*

P.I.X.A.L.'s voice interrupted his thoughts. "Zane, the program is glitching again. Be careful!"

*Bzzzzzzzzzzzzzz!* Zane fell back into the throne room, back to his first meeting with the Ice Emperor. Zane was once again pinned to the floor by ice, and the Ice Emperor stood over him, ready to finish him off.

"Zane, you have returned to your subconscious," P.I.X.A.L. told him. "Remember, this is not a memory. This is you, fighting yourself."

A feeling of calmness flowed through Zane. He knew what he was supposed to do.

Zane stared into the Ice Emperor's cruel eyes. "I forgive you," Zane said.

At the words, icy blue light swept through Zane's body. He felt the Elemental Power of Ice surge through his being. The ice shards pinning him to the floor shattered as he jumped to his feet.

"You cannot hurt me anymore. Me or anyone else!" Zane cried.

Thrusting his arms forward, he hurled a blast of ice at the Ice Emperor's right arm. The blast knocked

the Staff of Forbidden Spinjitzu from his hand. It clattered to the floor.

The Ice Emperor growled—and then stopped. He took off his helmet. His cold, hard face transformed back into the face of the Titanium Ninja. Finally, he was his old himself again.

"I think we are done here," he told Zane.

"I think so, too," Zane said. "P.I.X.A.L., I am ready to return!"

A blinding white light filled the throne room, and in the next instant, Zane's eyes fluttered open in the Samurai-X cave.

"Zane!" P.I.X.A.L. cried. She hurried to him and began to detach the sensors. "That glitch was very helpful," Zane said. "I found the answer I was looking for in my subconscious, when I was forced to battle myself. Look!"

He held out his hands, and in seconds, an ice sculpture of P.I.X.A.L. appeared on the floor in front of her.

She smiled. "I take it the experiment was a success, then."

"It was," Zane replied. "My Elemental Power of Ice has returned. I discovered that I needed to forgive myself. I could not move forward without accepting my past."

"I am glad it worked," P.I.X.A.L. said. "But I am afraid that it will be too dangerous to share this program with the others."

"I am sure that Cole, Jay, and Kai will find their own ways to regain their powers," Zane replied. "We may all have different lessons to learn. But one thing that we all know is that a ninja never quits!"

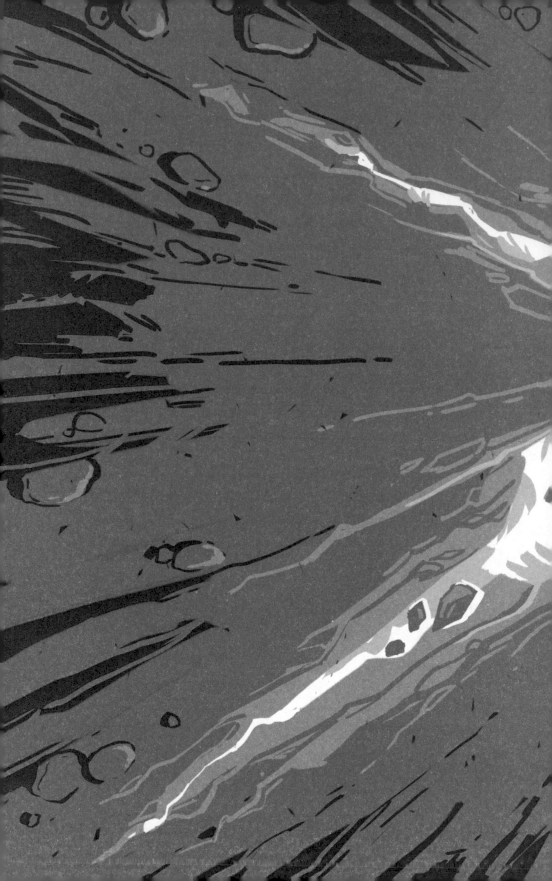

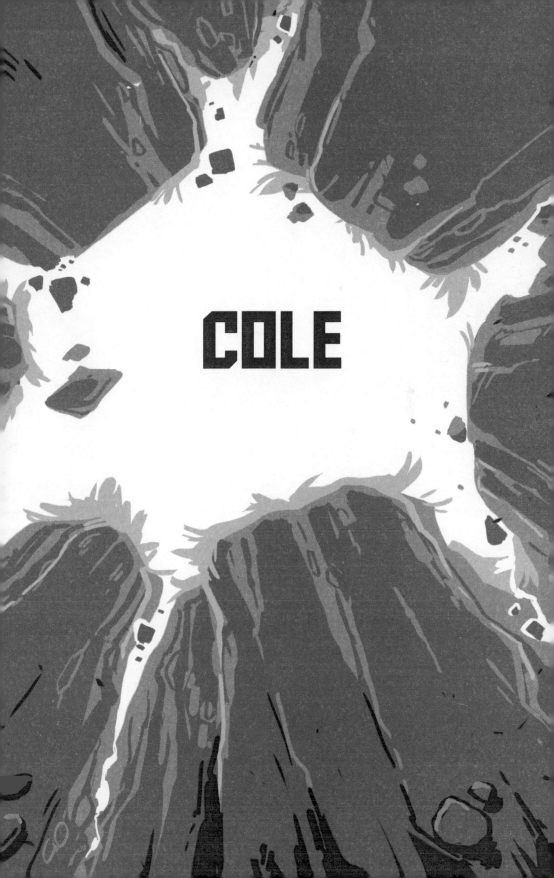

# Chapter One
# Down on the Farm

Carrying his suitcase, a dark-haired man with a neatly trimmed mustache walked across the rural road to the gate of a small farm. An older woman in overalls and a straw hat was using a hoe to break up soil.

"Excuse me," the man said. "I was wondering if you'd seen my son, Cole? Bushy eyebrows, great head of hair?"

"Yup," the woman drawled. "He's over yonder, tryin' to get Henry to plow the big field."

She turned and pointed past the rice paddies that ran along the side of the farm to the large field

behind the farmhouse. The man could see Cole straining to coax a fat yak into pulling a metal plow.

"You got yourself a good boy," the woman said. "But we ain't sure who's more stubborn, Cole or Henry."

The man smiled. "That sounds like Cole."

As she walked the man over, she noticed his suitcase was covered with stickers bearing city names. "You one o' them travelin' performers?"

"Yes," he replied, smiling proudly. "I'm part of a song-and-dance group called the Royal

Blacksmiths. You may have heard of us; we've won the Blade Cup several times."

"Nope, never heard of ya," she answered. "We don't have time for performers out here. . . . Crops don't take a night off, so we don't, either. My name's Sally-Bob, by the way."

"I'm Lou. Pleased to meet you," the man said.

As they drew closer, Lou watched Cole plant his hands on the yak's rear end and push as hard as he could, his feet slipping in mud. Henry seemed happy where he was. Lou also saw that Cole had a bandage around his head and bruises on his arms—like he'd been in a fight. But Lou didn't know how that would be possible. Since losing his power as Master of Earth in the battle against the Crystal King, Cole hadn't been in any fights that Lou knew of.

Cole's feet finally slid out from under him completely, and he plopped face-first into the mud. Henry grunted.

"Looking good, son," Lou said cheerily.

Cole looked up, wiping mud from his eyes, and broke into a huge smile. "Dad!" he cried, leaping up to hug his father and getting mud all over Lou's suit. "How did you find me?"

Lou squeezed his son back. "You wrote Master Wu a letter, remember?" Lou said. "To tell him where you'd be in case he ever needed you. It's been a while since we last saw each other, so I took a break between tour stops to come and see if you're all right. Losing your powers as the Master of Earth can't have been easy."

Sally-Bob turned to amble back to her field. "I'll leave you two to your huggin'," she said. "Crops don't hug, and neither do we. You're welcome to stay in our barn with your boy as long as you like," she told Lou.

"Thank you," Lou called back, waving. Then he noticed the mud all over his suit. He chuckled and started to wipe it off.

"Sorry about that," Cole muttered. "It's great to see you, Dad. But I'm fine. After I left the Monastery, I was pretty down, wondering what I was going to do with the rest of my life. All of my friends had moved on. I was just wandering. . . . I didn't feel . . . *anchored* to anything. Then I found this farm. And I thought, 'Master of Earth, farming the land . . .' It sorta made sense, so I thought I'd give it a try, and see what not fighting all the time would be like. But

enough about that. Come on, let's get you settled. Henry, you take a break."

The yak grunted again. Cole took his father's suitcase and led him past some small houses and toward a large barn. "And I kinda like it here. The people have treated me great, like one of their own," he said. He waved at a farmer walking in the other direction, carrying a sack of seeds. "Hi, Bob-Bob! Heading out to plant that north field?"

The man smiled and nodded, continuing on, and when he was past, Cole saw that his father was confused. "That's Bob-Bob," he explained to

Lou. "He's Sally-Bob's brother. That's one of the best things about this place—only some of the farmers are related to each other, but they all treat each other like one big family. And they're super peaceful. I think they worship the land."

Lou gently touched one of the bruises on Cole's arm. "Looks like peaceful farming can get pretty dangerous," he said.

"Oh, that," Cole replied with a frown. "Sally-Bob's bunch has been having trouble with her neighbor, Takanagi. He's a big-time farmer who owns all the land around Sally-Bob's, and Sally-Bob won't sell. Takanagi wants *all* the land, though,

so he sends his thugs over here every so often to try to 'convince' her."

"And you've been defending the land for the farmers," Lou guessed.

"Trying to, at least. I promised Mom I'd always stand up for others, and that means whether I have powers or not." He sighed. "I thought being here would be a simpler life, one where I didn't need to be a ninja. So far, that hasn't happened, but I think it will work out somehow eventually."

Lou nodded. Then he looked at Cole closely. "I know you say you like it here, but do you feel— what was the word you used?—'anchored' here?

Maybe 'grounded' is a better term. Like this place and these people give you a sense of balance in your life?"

Cole shrugged. "I don't know. I feel like something's been missing since I lost my powers, and working here makes it not so bad. At least, I don't think about it as much." Lou could hear the uncertainty in Cole's voice. He knew not feeling so bad wasn't the same as being grounded.

As they continued into the barn, Lou looked around. A farm was hardly the place he expected to find Cole. But if this was where his son really felt he should be, then so be it.

## Chapter Two
# Attack of the War-Tractors!

Lou woke with a start, sitting up in Sally-Bob's barn, hearing a groaning sound, like a heavy door opening for the first time in hundreds of years.

"What's that?!" he cried.

Across the barn, Cole woke and wiped sleep from his eyes. "Huh? Oh, that's the farm's rooster. It must be sunrise."

"That doesn't sound like any rooster I've ever heard," Lou replied, hurrying to the barn door and sliding it open. Instead of a rooster, he was startled to see the yak standing before him. It licked him

from chin to hairline with its sandpapery tongue. Lou yelped in surprise, jumping back.

"Henry likes to pretend he's a rooster," Cole explained, patting Henry's nose.

Lou looked at the dark sky. "But it doesn't look like the sun's coming up," he pointed out. "It *looks* like the middle of the night."

Cole stepped out of the barn with his dad and gazed at the stars, confused. "That's weird," he said. "The only other time Henry pretends he's a rooster is when there's trouble, but I don't see any—"

Before he could finish, they heard the rumbling

of engines, and a moment later, five pairs of headlights crested a hill in the distance. The lights grew bigger and the rumbling louder as they approached the farm.

"Takanagi?" Lou asked.

"Yeah . . . Stay here, Dad," Cole implored. "You'll be safe."

Cole ran toward the headlights. Whatever Takanagi was sending their way, there were more of them than there were of Cole. Lou admired his son's bravery, but he wished he had someone or something else on his side. The other farmers stood outside their homes, watching, not making any move to go to his aid. And Cole was trying to protect them! Maybe the farmers *were* peaceful, but surely they could do *something* to help! Since it appeared they wouldn't, Lou decided *he* would.

He ran after Cole, quickly becoming winded. *I'm in shape for soft-shoe dancing, not sprinting*, he thought. As he got closer, he saw that the approaching vehicles were tractors, which made sense, but they weren't like normal tractors. They had been heavily modified, with metal plating along their sides. The drivers, too, wore metal plating on their overalls. They

wore helmets and carried long pitchforks, like bizarre armored knights from some medieval tale.

Lou ran up beside his son, who had stopped to make a stand before the war-tractors.

"Dad! I told you to wait in the barn! You're not a fighter!" Cole exclaimed.

"I'll do whatever I can to protect my family," Lou replied firmly. "Family is the most important thing."

The drivers stopped their war-tractors. The lead driver pointed his pitchfork handle at Cole. "Save

yourself a lot more pain, kid, and convince Sally-Bob to sell to Takanagi!"

"I've told you: this is *their* land, and if they don't want to sell, they don't have to!"

The lead driver turned to his partners and waved them ahead.

"Do you have a plan, son?" Lou asked worriedly.

"Since I don't have my powers, I'll just keep doing what I've been doing: using my Spinjitzu and hoping for the best," Cole told him.

The war-tractors were already almost upon them. Cole tried to spin but didn't have enough room, and he turned right into the broom handles of two of the drivers. He fell, adding more bruises to his collection. Two other drivers, grinning, circled Cole at high speed, splashing mud all over him.

The fifth driver sped straight at Lou. Lou didn't know quite what to do. He didn't know any fancy fighting moves, just dance steps.

Suddenly, he realized what he *could* do, and he smiled. Just as the war-tractor reached him, Lou gracefully slid to one side. As the machine went past, Lou executed a perfect dance twirl, his foot connecting with the war-tractor at the perfect time in the perfect spot . . . at least, that was what Lou was hoping for. But instead of knocking the heavy vehicle on its side as he had intended, Lou just bounced awkwardly off the machine and landed very *un*gracefully in the mud! The driver was speechless—absolutely baffled by what he had witnessed—and couldn't take his eyes off the unfortunate dancer. He was so preoccupied with Lou's blunder, he didn't notice he was driving his vehicle off the path and straight into a ditch until it was too late. The war-tractor suddenly fell over on its side, sending its driver into the mud, too.

Cole, however, was having a lot more trouble. Three of the other drivers wouldn't allow him a moment so he could use his Spinjitzu. He concentrated on deflecting their blows instead, but the fourth driver swooped his pitchfork handle behind Cole's knees, and he fell once more.

The three drivers broke away, rampaging their war-tractors up and down the fields, ruining the farmers' crops. The farmers still just watched. Cole again tried to stand, but the leader pinned him to the ground with his pitchfork handle.

"This was your last chance, kid. Next time, we'll get *mean*."

The goons all turned and drove back the way they'd come, having done enough damage for now.

Lou looked at his dazed son with concern. "Cole, are you all right?"

"No broken bones," Cole replied, rising unsteadily with Lou's help. He watched the thugs go, his eyes distant.

Lou worried for him. "What is it, Cole?" he said.

Cole didn't look back at him. "It's just . . . I don't know how I'm going to do it, this time," he told his father. "I don't know how I can keep my promise to Mom."

## Chapter Three
# The Living Room Dance

Lou stayed up all night with Cole outside the barn, listening to his son try to come up with a plan for defeating Takanagi and his thugs, then throwing away his ideas almost as soon as he thought of them. When morning arrived, Cole was no closer to a solution.

"The more I fight back against him for the farmers, the more violent he's going to get . . . and with the farmers not being fighters, they could get really hurt!" he said. "But if I leave, they'll lose their land and I'll be breaking my promise to Mom."

Suddenly, Lou had a thought. "What if we put on a show to distract Takanagi and his henchmen?"

*"Okaaaay,"* Cole said slowly, asking a question he already knew the answer to. "What happens when the show's over?"

Lou thought about it, then slumped. "The farmers would be right back where they started."

"I feel powerless," Cole said through clenched teeth, frustrated. "I mean, I know I don't have any powers, but I hate *feeling* powerless." He looked down. "I bet Mom never felt this way."

"You'd be wrong," Lou told him. Cole looked up, surprised.

"It wasn't long after your mother and I met that she unlocked her True Potential. She had some amazing adventures. We were young and in love, and soon we decided to have the biggest adventure together—becoming parents. Lilly was so excited, knowing she'd pass her powers on to her child—*you.*"

Cole smiled. He'd never heard this story about his mother before. Other farmers, including Sally-Bob, started wandering over to listen, too.

"After you were born," Lou went on, "your mom kept going out on missions. She loved helping others. But those missions became bigger, and she'd be away for more and more time. I felt guilty because I wasn't helping her. I questioned why she had me in her life at all. How could she need a powerless man like me?"

"So what did ya do?" Sally-Bob asked, thoroughly engrossed in the story.

"Well, I knew *Cole* needed me," Lou said, then turned back to his son. "I took some time off from the Royal Blacksmiths so I could always be around, even when your Mom couldn't. And you and I had a wonderful time, playing together, singing together, dancing in the living room . . . One day, your mother came home from a long adventure— she had just saved all of Ninjago—and she was crying."

"Why?" Cole asked, leaning forward.

"Because you'd grown so much, and she felt like she hadn't been a part of any of it. She *had* spent time with you, but not as much as she'd wanted. She said she was feeling very out of balance. It was starting to affect her during missions. She was thinking about us when she was out fighting, and when she was with us, she was thinking about how

to be a better hero. She didn't feel grounded in either place."

"She felt powerless," Cole said quietly.

"Exactly," Lou said. "But you and I looked at each other and—it was amazing—we took her hands and started dancing with her . . . right there in the living room. And we laughed and we cried happy tears because we were together. Your mom knew we were okay, that we were always thinking of her and loving her, and that she could draw strength from family. And I finally knew that I was helping her. I knew she needed me, because I— *we*—kept her grounded. Family was the foundation for everything. She carried that with her the rest of her days."

Lou smiled at his son. "We all feel powerless sometimes. So it's good to know we can draw strength from our families if we need to."

"Wow . . . Thanks for telling me that, Dad. I wish she was here right now. It's awesome that *you're* here, but I could really use all the strength I can get against Takanagi. Especially since Sally-Bob and her friends aren't fighters."

"Says who?" Sally-Bob asked indignantly.

"Huh?" Cole said, surprised and confused. "I just assumed . . . Because you never try to help me when Takanagi's thugs come . . ."

Sally-Bob scowled at him. "You never asked. You just came in here and you told us to stay back, that you'd handle it. So we did."

Cole squeezed his eyes shut, embarrassed. "You're kidding!" he exclaimed.

"Crops don't kid, so we don't, either," Sally-Bob informed him. "But we *will* learn how to fight to defend our land . . . if you show us how."

Optimism and excitement surged through Cole. "Let's get started!" he shouted.

"Not just yet," Sally-Bob said, leaning down and squinting at him. "One more thing you need to know, fella. The minute you planted your first seed here, you became part of *our* family, too."

Cole smiled gratefully. So did his father. "Yes, ma'am!" Cole replied.

## Chapter Four
# The Battle of Sally-Bob's Farm

The rest of that day and the early part of the evening were spent on training. Cole gave the farmers a crash course in farm defense, using whatever was at hand for makeshift weapons. He held tryouts to see who could throw a corncob the farthest and the hardest. Sally-Bob had a surprisingly good arm. He instructed the farmers how to use hoes as combat staves in case the struggle became hand-to-hand.

That went fine, although the farmers with shorter attention spans kept wandering off to dig furrows that could be used later for planting. Cole cleverly redirected their efforts so they were digging deep trenches in which to hide—or trap Takanagi's war-tractors.

Together, they all pitched in to tear down the barn, repurposing its wooden planks and tools to construct primitive catapults that were nonetheless capable of launching hay bales several hundred feet. Lou participated in the training as well, hoping maybe he could learn a little something that, if not useful for fighting, might come in handy as, perhaps, a dance move.

When training was over, Cole knew it wouldn't be enough to stop Takanagi and his men. The farmers simply didn't have enough firepower to hold out against the invaders. But he hoped desperately that if Sally-Bob and the others could stand strong enough and maybe get in a few licks on Takanagi, he, like most bullies, might decide they were too much trouble and leave them alone.

"Are you ready?" Lou asked quietly, after all the preparations had been made. He and Cole crouched behind Sally-Bob's house in the last light of the day. The other farmers hid behind their own homes or crouched in newly dug trenches. Sally-Bob was with her neighbor behind his house.

"I think so," Cole answered finally. "But can I tell you something strange?"

"You can tell me anything," Lou replied.

"I feel more like the way I was—more like myself—than I have since I lost my powers. You know how you were talking about being grounded? I think that's kind of how I feel. . . . Maybe not by this specific place, but by these people. Does that make sense?"

"Absolutely," Lou told him.

Cole sighed. "I just hope all this work today wasn't for nothing. I mean, we don't even know if Takanagi is coming tonight."

Lou looked beyond the farm's property line and pointed. "I don't think you have to worry about that," he said. The headlights were back at the top of the hill, and Cole could make out the war-tractors' silhouettes.

One man stepped in between two of the war-tractors. His armor was different from the others'. He spoke into a megaphone. "This is Takanagi! I do not appreciate having to be here, but I wanted

you to see the face of the man who will seize your land! With my control of this whole region, everyone will come to me for their vegetables, and I will make them pay whatever I want! Do not resist my forces! I have another weapon besides these. . . . I do not wish to use it. It is even more horrible and destructive!" He paused, running through a mental checklist. "Okay, I think that is everything! Here we come!"

The war-tractors began moving down the hill.

"Just the way you thought they'd do this," Lou said to Cole, who nodded.

Takanagi's forces approached a seemingly flat patch of land leading into Sally-Bob's farm, but when they tried to cross it, the planks dusted with cut grass disguising the empty trench beneath gave way. With a loud *WHOOMPF,* the war-tractors fell nose-first, throwing their drivers forward to land on the trench's bottom.

There was a cheer from behind the other houses as the farmers realized that their defense strategy worked. But the drivers clumsily scaled the trench in their heavy armor, leaving behind their war-tractors and lumbering forward on foot.

Cole waved his hand to signal the farmers, who stepped out of hiding and began hurling their projectiles—corncobs, heads of bok choy, and potatoes they had grown. Many missed their mark, but thanks to their armor, the thugs were too heavy to dodge others (most of which were thrown by Sally-Bob). None did any real damage, but several of the goons overbalanced and fell on impact. They would get up only to be knocked down again. Cole could see them looking at each other with confusion and even fear. What *else* could the farmers have back there to use against them? After their fifth failed attempt to advance, the exhausted goons chose to turn and run back the way they'd come.

But before the farmers could celebrate, there was another, louder roar from the top of the hill. Everyone turned, and to their horror, they saw an even larger armored vehicle, this time a massive harvester, rumbling toward them. Suddenly, it belched a plume of flame!

"I don't think the corncobs are going to do too much against that," Sally-Bob said worriedly as the war-harvester growled across the fields, coming straight for where the group was standing.

"That's why we have the catapults," Cole replied grimly. "Get ready to launch!"

The farmers ran to their positions by the catapults, which were already loaded with hay bales, and let fly. The projectiles arced toward the war-thresher . . . but they either smashed harmlessly against its sides or they were incinerated by jets of flame.

The war-thresher continued its slow advance as Cole, Lou, and the farmers watched. Cole could feel the eyes of the farmers and his father on him, waiting for his orders. There was only one left he could think to give that might do any good. He turned to them. "I don't want any of you to get hurt. I'll hold Takanagi off as long as I can while you get to safety. Run!"

Not giving them a chance to protest, Cole turned back around and started marching toward the oncoming war-thresher. He had no idea what he was going to do. But then, out of the corners of his eyes, he could see Sally-Bob, the farmers, and even Lou walking with him!

"What are you doing?" he asked in panic. "I told you to run!"

"Crops don't run, and neither do we," Sally-Bob growled in response. "We stand up for our land . . . like the family we are."

They kept marching. Whatever they would do, they'd do it together.

The final, terrible resolution seemed inevitable . . . until the last member of the farm family took matters into his own hooves. Henry the yak lumbered in front of the farmers and into the path of the harvester, then simply stood there. The harvester paused, as if unsure what to do.

"We need a distraction to get Takanagi away from Henry before that thresher turns him into steak," Lou said. He grabbed up three leftover potatoes, then ran across the field.

"Dad, don't!" Cole yelled, running after him.

But Lou ran to a spot about fifty feet to Henry's left . . . and started dancing the fanciest soft-shoe he knew, while juggling the potatoes! He spun, he twirled, he leapt. In the war-harvester, Takanagi sat mesmerized by the impromptu performance. Who was this fool, defending a stubborn yak? Then he remembered why he was there. Angry at himself, he pushed the button to restart the flamethrower and turned it toward the Royal Blacksmith.

*Guess there'll be no curtain call,* Lou thought, bracing himself.

Just before the flamethrower could turn him into ash, however, Cole tackled his father, pushing him out of the way. The flame jet roared over their heads!

"That was a crazy move, Dad!" he said, impressed by his father's bravery.

"A good performer knows how to improvise," Lou gasped, out of breath.

They heard the war-thresher rumble past them and past Henry, again trundling toward the farm . . . and the farmers, who stood fearlessly as the very last line of defense.

"Move!" Cole yelled desperately, waving his arms in hopes of getting the farmers' attention. "Get away from there, people! Come on! You're going to get hurt!"

But if the farmers heard him, they showed no sign. They did not turn and run. Instead, they planted their feet firmly and did something unexpected: they joined hands.

When Cole saw this, he was amazed . . . and then he felt a strange surge within him—adrenaline! But there was also something more. Something . . . powerful. And oddly familiar. When Cole saw the farmers standing together and supporting each

other, he mustered the emotional strength he'd lost during fight with the Crystal King.

Energy shot through his limbs, and his heart thrummed in his chest. Pointing his hands toward the war-harvester and smiling, he wondered if he'd regained anything else he had lost. But he was pretty sure he knew the answer. Just as power coursed in his veins like lava ready to explode from a volcano, a column of rock erupted beneath the war-harvester, flipping it into the air and sending it flying away from the farmers.

His confidence soaring, Cole gestured just as the war-harvester landed. Before Takanagi could take any action, another earthen pillar sent the vehicle flying backward once more, then again and again, until it disappeared over the hill! The farmers celebrated, jumping up and down, whooping and hollering. Lou hugged his son.

"Your powers! They're back! You restored your balance and unlocked your True Potential again! How did you do it?"

"*You* did it, Dad . . . By telling me that story about Mom and how we gave her strength when we held hands and danced in the living room. Seeing the farmers hold hands, supporting each other and grounding each other . . . I think it grounded *me* again."

Lou nodded. "Because you care about these people. Just like you've become part of their family, they've become part of yours. And family *is* strength!" He put his hand on his son's shoulder, filled with emotion. "You were amazing today, but with or without your powers, you've always made your mother—and me—very proud."

Cole and Lou grinned as the farmers rushed to them, slapping Cole on the back. "I have to say, your powers came back with a real sense of timing!" Lou said with a wink. "You must get it from your dad!"

## Chapter Five
# One Last Obstacle

Cole and Lou stayed at the farm a while longer and helped rebuild the barn and plant new crops. During that time, Takanagi never returned, nor was he seen at all. After a few days, they heard good news—Takanagi had, in fact, sold all his land because he'd decided it was "too much trouble," and was headed far away to pursue a different empire in "something easier . . . like pillowcases." Cole's prediction about a bully's behavior had proven true. Much relieved, the farmers dreamed of having a bumper crop the next harvest season, and using the profits to buy all the land Takanagi once had, so they could start their own vegetable empire.

When the barn was done, Sally-Bob saw Cole and Lou approaching, carrying their bags. "You'll be leaving now, I expect."

"The Royal Blacksmiths have some big shows coming up," Lou told them with a smile. "But when we come back this way, I'll make sure there are tickets for you."

"Well, crops don't go to shows, and neither do we." Sally-Bob smiled at Lou. "But in your case, I reckon we could make an exception."

She turned to Cole. "You goin' on the road with your dad?"

Lou looked at Cole, too. He'd wondered the same thing.

"I'm going back to the Monastery of Spinjitzu," Cole said. "If I've rediscovered my True Potential and my powers are back, that may have happened for the other ninja, too. If so, maybe it's time to become a team again. But I'll never forget my time here, Sally-Bob, and how you helped me feel balanced and grounded again. If Takanagi—or anyone else—ever threatens you, send word to the Monastery and I'll come help."

"I reckon we won't need you for that," Sally Bob said, "now that you've taught us how to stick up for ourselves. But if you're free around harvest time . . ."

Cole laughed. "I'll be here."

They all shook hands, and Cole and Lou walked toward the gate. "I'm glad we got to spend some time together, son," Lou said.

Cole put an arm around his Dad's shoulders. "Me too, Dad. You know, you're as much of a hero as Mom was."

"Oh no, I'm just a song-and-dance man who can juggle a little," Lou said, modestly.

"I'm serious. By keeping Mom grounded, you brought her balance and strength so *she* could be the hero she needed to be. In part because of you, she was able to help a lot of people she wouldn't have been able to otherwise. That means *you* helped them, too."

"I guess I never thought about it like that," Lou said, embarrassed. "Thank you, Cole . . . But is it okay if I leave the fighting part of being a hero to people like you?"

They walked a few more steps, laughing. Then Cole noticed something ahead. "Looks like we forgot to say goodbye to somebody."

Henry the yak stood between them and the gate, chewing some grass. He was acting as if he wasn't looking at them, but Cole had a feeling the yak was intentionally blocking them. Cole walked up and patted Henry on his flank.

"Henry, old buddy, I'm going to miss you," Cole told the animal. "But I'll see you soon, for harvest."

Henry moved a few steps to the side, allowing them access to the gate. Now he was looking Lou straight in the eye.

"I think he wants you to say goodbye, too, Dad," said Cole.

"Really? Well, okay . . ." He walked up to Henry's snout, unsure of what to say. "Well, Henry, I guess—"

But before he could get another word out, Henry licked his face again with his slobbery tongue, covering him in yak drool. Cole laughed as Lou wiped his face with his sleeve. Lou was laughing, too.

"You're a funny yak, Henry," said Lou. "You ever think about going on the road and performing?"

Lou and Cole walked out the gate and down the road together. Henry grunted and moved over to another patch of grass and went on with his day.

## Chapter One
# The Getaway

"Welcome to paradise!" Nya said gleefully, setting down her bag. The plush hotel room's furniture was overstuffed, the carpeting thick, and the towels soft. And she was sure that Jay's room next door was just as nice. "I love this new resort already . . . and hardly anyone's even heard about this island! No video games, no television, an all-you-can-eat buffet at every meal . . . just peace and quiet!"

Getting no response, she turned to see Jay staring out the glass door to the balcony. Past that, there was nothing but lush jungle. He hadn't even dropped his backpack. "Jay?" she said. He still didn't turn around. "Jay!"

He jumped, startled, and smiled weakly. "Sorry, Nya," he said. "I was somewhere else."

"Well, hurry up and get here," Nya replied. She sat on the bed and bounced on it a little to see how comfortable it was. Jay walked over stiffly and sat. "Come on, Jay, we thought this would be an amazing vacation for us after the fight with the Crystal King. Aside from other guests, we're literally as far as we could possibly get from everything."

"I know," Jay said, sounding a little guilty. "And it really is beautiful."

"So it should be perfect for us to relax, rest up and . . . adjust, right?" Nya asked gently.

"You're right. I'm sorry, Nya," he said again. "I just feel like . . . like I'm missing a piece of myself."

Nya stood up, nodding with understanding. "Well, yeah. You're missing the powers you had as Master of Lightning."

Jay stood, too, and walked back to the balcony doors. "The way I'm feeling is like when I think about my birth mom giving me up to the Walkers for adoption. I love Ed and Edna—they *are* my parents—but I'm always going to have this hole inside where my real mother should be."

"Hey, getting used to the changes in your life will take a while, and that's okay," Nya said. "I just want you to get back to being *you*, you know? You haven't cracked a single bad joke since we left the Monastery."

He turned around, an exaggerated look of hurt on his face. "Wait. My jokes are *bad*?"

Nya smiled and gave him a playful punch on the arm. "That's more like it. Why don't you take a walk around, explore, and try not to think about your birth mom, or your powers, or . . . or anything. When you come back, we'll hit that buffet!"

Jay looked dubious. "Walk around?" He gestured to the dense foliage outside their room. "Outside?"

"You don't have to walk into the jungle, city boy. The beach is on the opposite side of the resort. Stay on the hotel grounds and you'll be fine," Nya reassured him. As he walked toward the door, she added, "But come back, all right? Don't run off to some lighthouse, paint really bad paintings, and become a hermit again."

"Don't worry; been there, done that," Jay answered, smiling. Then his face took on that comically hurt expression again. "Wait. My paintings were *bad*?"

Nya laughed, relieved that Jay's sense of humor, at least, seemed to be coming back, however slowly. "Get lost," she told him with mock sternness.

Jay smiled and walked out.

## Chapter Two
# Lost and Found

"I am hopelessly lost," Jay said five minutes later, standing in the jungle.

He'd been walking the path around the resort's swimming pool, where kids frolicked and a man played steel drums. The next thing Jay knew, the pool was nowhere to be seen and the jungle had surrounded him.

It was Jay's own fault; the walk hadn't cleared his mind at all. He couldn't stop thinking about how similar it felt to not have his powers and to not know the reasons his mother, from whom he'd inherited those powers, gave him up. *I guess they're both about loss,* he thought. *I'll never get either one back.*

Jay paused and strained his ears, trying to hear some sound that could lead him back to the hotel. But there was nothing—no children splashing in the pool, no tropical music from the steel drum player. There was no way he could contact Nya or the hotel.

Jay turned in a circle. "All these plants look alike," he moaned. Then he gulped. "I wonder if venomous frogs are hiding under them, just waiting to pounce on me and make *me* part of

their all-they-can-eat buffet. . . . How embarrassing would that be? Surviving the Crystal King only to be taken out by a toad with a rumbly tummy . . ."

He took a deep breath. "It's okay, Jay," he told himself. "Your imagination is just running away with you. You can't be that far from the hotel, and you haven't been walking that long . . . It only *seems* like forever. You'll just look up, see where the sun is, and you'll know what time it is and what direction you're heading in." Jay looked up through the canopy of leaves overhead, but the leaves were all he could see. He groaned, then realized something. "You know you're on an island. If you walk in a straight line, sooner or later you'll come to a coastline, and you'll just follow it around the island until you reach the hotel. And you won't think about hungry, ninja-eating frogs." Jay nodded confidently to himself and started walking. Nothing bad was going to happen.

▣▭▣

"This is bad," Jay said five minutes later, finding himself trapped in a thicket of thornbushes.

And the four minutes before that hadn't been great, either: Jay had stepped on a pile of fallen leaves and found they covered a deep hole with slick, muddy sides that proved tricky to crawl out of; he'd walked through a cloud of gnats, who stung him approximately four million times; and he'd surprised two wild boars with very sharp tusks, who had then chased him . . . into the thornbushes.

"Okay," he mused, "at least the boars are gone. Now the key is to stay calm."

Jay stayed calm for about three seconds, then thrashed like mad, only to become more and more entangled. Finally, he stopped, breathing hard.

*"I think I'll take a nice walk,"* he sneered, exaggerating his own voice. *"Maybe it'll help me clear my head.* That's the last time I listen to myself. . . ."

But then he heard something approaching.

"Are those footsteps?" he wondered aloud, then frowned. "I hope they're not boar-hoof-steps."

Then he heard the sound again. Definitely footsteps!

"Help!" he cried out. "Over here!"

Jay heard the footsteps speed up, coming closer.

"That's it! This way!" Jay urged. A moment later, he heard something hacking through thick vines, and thanks to his imagination running wild once more, he suddenly worried that he'd stumbled into the territory of a fiendish fugitive who'd been hiding on this remote island with nothing but a large machete for company. But finally, the last branches between Jay and his rescuer were removed, and Jay found himself staring into the face of . . . not a bloodthirsty criminal, but—

"Unagami?"

The formerly threatening artificial intelligence from the *Prime Empire* video game, now in the form of a young boy, folded up the walking stick he'd been using to clear brush and put it in his kids' backpack,

which was decorated with star fighters and big-headed aliens.

"Hi, Jay!" Unagami said, waving at Jay cheerfully. "Wow! How crazy is it that we're both here on the same island, in the same jungle, face to face?"

"I promise to try to figure that out after you help me get out of these thorns," Jay grunted.

As Unagami removed snagged branches from Jay's sleeves, Jay looked at the boy with confusion. "What are you doing here, anyway?"

"Well," Unagami began, "since the last you saw me—"

"When you looked totally different and were the vengeful ruler of Prime Empire, trying to destroy me and my friends," Jay reminded him.

"That's true," Unagami agreed sheepishly. "But I've grown up a lot since then."

Jay raised an eyebrow. Either Unagami ignored him or didn't notice.

"Anyway, I've been spending a lot of time with my father, the man who created me, Milton Dyer. We've been getting to know each other and becoming a family. I've never felt so happy, so . . . complete!"

"Good for you," Jay growled, remembering his own situation.

"But I've also been developing a new game that happens in a hidden city in a jungle on a remote island," said Unagami, smiling proudly. "I'm here doing research! There are rumors of a city like that right here on this island! Do you want to help me look for it?"

"I guess it's better than getting lost again trying to find my way back to the hotel," Jay grumbled.

"What did you say?" Unagami asked.

"Nothing," Jay answered quickly. He knew Nya would be starting to wonder where he was. But finding a lost city sounded like a lot of fun . . . certainly more than thinking about his inner emptiness.

"I'd love to help you look," he told Unagami. "Thanks."

"Awesome!" Unagami exclaimed. "Before we get going, I just want to call my dad and tell him I ran into you! He'll be so surprised!"

Jay watched as Unagami took a tablet device from his backpack and turned it on. An icon of the boy's face appeared, blinking, as it booted up. "I call this the Unaga-Meeting Pad! It makes calls from anywhere to anywhere else and it's powered by our planet's magnetic field! I invented it yesterday! Pretty awesome, right?"

"Gee," Jay replied sarcastically. "Getting to know your dad, creating a new game, revolutionizing communications . . . What are you doing in all your spare time, Unagami? Figuring out why the chicken crossed the road?"

"No," Unagami replied, dialing. "I started to, but then I realized it wasn't any of my business."

Jay thought about that, then had to nod. It was a good answer.

A moment later, the holographic face of Milton Dyer appeared. "Hi, Dad! It's so good to see you! You'll never guess who I'm with right now!"

*So much for not thinking about my inner emptiness*, Jay thought gloomily.

## Chapter Three
# Buried Treasure

After walking for two hours, following a blurry, torn map that a whistling Unagami had produced from his backpack, he and Jay were back in the exact same spot where Unagami had rescued the former Master of Lightning. At least, that's what it looked like to Jay, who had had enough and stopped in his tracks.

"Okay, I'm tired, I'm hungry, I'm itchy, and I'm sweaty," he told Unagami. "And you've been whistling the same song over and over!"

"I know," Unagami replied happily. "Isn't it awesome?"

A coconut fell from a tree somewhere above, thudding heavily at Jay's feet, narrowly missing his head. Jay retrieved the coconut and held it up for Unagami to see.

"And I've almost been beaned by sixteen coconuts!" He was also tired of reliving in his mind how he'd lost his powers, or how he'd learned that his birth mother had given him up for adoption, though Jay didn't mention any of that. Oh, and Unagami had made three more phone calls to Milton Dyer, "just to say hello."

"Are we getting any closer to this 'lost city' of yours?" Jay asked crankily. "My feet feel like we've already walked a million miles."

"The coconut might help with your hunger issues, and we've actually traveled a mile and a half from where we started," Unagami informed him, looking at his digital watch. "And the journey can be as fun as the discovery!"

"Aw, you're just a kid," Jay muttered. "What do you know?"

"I'm a kid with an IQ in the tens of thousands," Unagami pointed out. Then he asked, out of genuine curiosity "Do you know what yours is?"

Jay, who did know his IQ, which was several tens of thousands lower than Unagami's, changed the subject quickly.

"Let's keep going," he said, "and see if this journey gets any more fun."

Unagami startled Jay by leaping toward him and bouncing his chest against Jay's. "Yes! That's the spirit! Wow, I'm sure having an awesome time hanging out with you!"

"Yeah, awesome . . . ," Jay said in response. But he couldn't help but smile as they started walking again. Unagami was a pesky and annoying know-it-all, but Jay found himself starting to like the kid nonetheless. It was hard to think of him as the terrible enemy he'd been not long before. Then, Unagami had been terribly unhappy, and was taking that unhappiness out on everyone and everything around him. But now he seemed positive and optimistic. Something inside him really had changed, and apparently for good.

Unagami turned the map in his hand and peered at it. "According to our map, the last landmark we need to see before finding the lost city is an unusual rock formation." He showed Jay the map, and the sketch on it of a stone shaped like a lightning bolt—a sharp diagonal interrupted by a horizontal middle. It appeared covered with greenery. Jay had never seen anything like it before.

"Well, something like that shouldn't be too hard to spot," he said, looking up, trying to see a break in the trees above. "There've gotta be some big mountains on this island with huge boulders, right? Where can we get a better view?"

Keeping his eyes trained on the jungle canopy, Jay started to walk back into the overgrowth.

"Be careful," Unagami urged, hurrying to keep up with him. "The jungle can be dangerous!"

"Aw, what do you know? You're just a kid," Jay repeated, then tripped over a vine and fell hard on his face.

"Jay! Are you all right?"

"I'm fine," he muttered. "Just wondering why lost cities are always in jungles and not in places I'm familiar with, like city parks."

Unagami tapped his chin, thinking. "I guess it would be because a lost city would likely be discovered if it were in a developed area, like a—"

"Lightning bolt!" Jay exclaimed suddenly.

"No, lightning bolts aren't developed, Jay,"
Unagami said patiently. "I think that's a pretty
obvious—"

"Lightning bolt! Look!"

Unagami looked down and saw Jay staring at
a rock the size of a shoe. It was a diagonal rock
jammed into the dirt at its narrowest point, but a
horizontal plane interrupted it halfway down, just
like in the sketch on Unagami's map.

"Yes! You found it, Jay!" Unagami enthused,
slapping him on the back and sending him sprawling
face-first into the dirt once more. Unagami looked

the rock over, and noticed that the half of it that caught any sunlight at all was greenish in hue.

Unagami gasped. "And look! It's covered in moss!"

"Huh," Jay said as he sat up, rubbing his chin. "Well, now that we found it, what next?"

Unagami turned the map over, but it was blank on the other side. "I don't know. This was the last of my reference material on the hidden city's location. Maybe we could walk in the direction it's pointing?"

The boy started walking the way the top of the rock was indicating, but Jay stopped him.

"Hang on, I bet you're going to want this as a souvenir," he said, yanking the rock out of the ground. As soon as he did, there was a loud rumbling noise, and the ground began to shake!

"What is it?" he shrieked. "A tidal wave? A tsunami?"

"No," Unagami shouted in response, "and those are the same thing! Look!"

He pointed at the ground. At the precise spot where the point of the rock had been, a long, straight crack formed in the earth, and then the

ground pulled back just wide enough that they could see stone stairs descending into darkness! When it was fully open, the rumbling and shaking ceased.

"You were right again, Jay! The rock *was* pointing to the hidden city! Only it was pointing *down*, not up!"

Jay smiled in wonder. "That's twice I've been looking at the sky when I should have been paying attention to what was right in front of me," he said. "I think there's probably a lesson in that."

But he was talking to empty air. Unagami was already headed down the stairs. Still clutching the lightning bolt rock, Jay followed him.

## Chapter Four
# Secrets in the Dark

Using a flashlight from his backpack, Unagami illuminated the long, long stairway as they walked, passing ancient, unused mounts for torches on the walls.

"Jay, when I found you trapped in those thorns," Unagami asked, "why hadn't you used your lightning powers to free yourself?"

"I don't have those powers anymore," he admitted. "And while I'm not sure how much I miss them, I do know that I don't feel complete without them."

"Yeah," Unagami replied. "I felt the same way until my dad and I figured some things out and started communicating better."

"Well, I can't communicate with powers, so it's kind of different," Jay pointed out.

"Maybe it's not *so* different," Unagami countered. "The chances of my father and I rebuilding our relationship were pretty slim. Just like you and I meeting on this island wasn't very likely. But both things happened. And nothing is truly lost forever. For example, this city we are searching for . . . The tribe that lived there was long thought gone forever. And yet we are about to find them, in a way. My father always says, you should never give in to the darkness of despair when there's still a flicker of possibility."

Jay had to smile again. The kid had some good points, but he wasn't about to admit it. "Aw, what do you know? You're just a kid," he said jokingly.

The stairs ended in a large, flat cave that Jay figured was some kind of meeting room, maybe to prepare for visits to the surface. A storage space had been carved into one wall, and it held wooden staffs that could be lit and used as torches.

In another storage space, they found longer staffs: spears. A clear blue stream of water ran like a tiny river through the chamber from the slightest crack under one wall, branching into all the exits ahead of them.

"Cool," Unagami noted. "They had their own water source, so all they had to gather was food!"

They explored the many caves that led away from this largest one and found what they thought must be living quarters, a community dining area, and even some kind of temple. But one long tunnel halted at a dead end: a stone wall covered top to bottom with etchings and carved spaces into which properly fitted pieces had been placed.

"I can't make heads or tails of this," Jay said.

"Early Ninjago language," Unagami answered, studying them closely. "I think this is a kind of welcome mat. It was written just before the tribe left the island, for whatever reason."

"They didn't leave much behind," Jay said, looking around. "That doesn't help your game idea much."

Unagami frowned. "It seems like there should be more to read about the tribe, but I don't see where . . ." Then he noticed something at the bottom of the wall and waved Jay over. "Jay! Do you still have the rock that led us to the entrance?"

Jay handed the rock to Unagami, and watched him slide it into a carved-out space in the wall that was shaped just like a lightning bolt! The wall trembled, as the entrance had done on the surface, and then the entire wall swung ninety degrees from its middle. There was a hiss of escaping old air as Jay and Unagami looked into an even larger chamber. In this one, there were recesses that had been carved into all the walls, and they were filled with neatly rolled scrolls.

"The tribe's library." Unagami's voice was almost a whisper.

"Way to go, Unagami!" Jay shouted, and the two of them, grinning, executed another chest bump.

This time, they both participated. "This treasure-hunting stuff is cool! I can see why people make movies about it!"

"I'm glad you're having fun," Unagami said, almost shyly. "I'm glad we're doing this together."

"Me too, buddy," Jay admitted.

"'Buddy,'" Unagami repeated. "I like that. No one's ever called me that before. I like it. It feels like something an older brother might say to a little brother."

Jay smiled in response, and he and Unagami practically tiptoed into the chamber, as if overly concerned with damaging or disturbing anything. Jay watched as Unagami delicately plucked out a scroll, unrolled it, and read it. When he was finished, he rolled it back up and replaced it, then took another. He nodded, reading, and gestured around the room.

"It looks like these scrolls are grouped by subject," Unagami said. "These have to do with food—how they found it, how they cooked it, and stuff like that. Some of the species they hunted for food have been extinct for a long time! These scrolls are thousands of years old!"

"Amazing," Jay said with awe.

Unagami hurried to another collection of scrolls and opened one.

"These explain how the tribe raised children," he said. "This is really interesting!"

"How so?"

"Every child born into the tribe was raised by the whole tribe, not just their mom and dad. Everyone shared equally in teaching the child and giving them all the things any parent could: care, love, education, protection, encouragement, discipline, and acceptance."

Unagami looked up sadly.

"I never had anyone to teach me those things or show them to me when I first became self-aware," he continued. "No wonder I was so unhappy!" His expression brightened. "It's a good thing that now my dad gives me all those things!"

Jay frowned when he felt himself realizing something.

"Wait . . . I had all those things when I was growing up. The parents who adopted me, Master Wu, the other ninja, all the friends I've made over the years . . . They did all the things for me that biological parents would have." He felt something in his chest loosening, a weight coming off his shoulders.

"And it is logical to believe you have given back to them the same things," Unagami said gently.

"Because ninja sharpens ninja," Jay went on, starting to smile. "My real mom must have known when she and my dad gave me to the Walkers that they'd make sure I'd always have people around me who would help me, guide me, and teach me. Powerless or not, they'd make sure I'd never be alone if I needed help!"

Even as he said it, he could feel warmth bloom in his chest and spread throughout his body. Then he felt a powerful jolt of energy spring from his chest and out to his hands. He looked at them in wonder. They were sparking! He could feel the hair on the back of his neck and on his arms stand up. It was a familiar feeling, and his heart began to race. He felt stronger and more alive than he'd felt in weeks. Jay felt himself smiling, and Unagami was looking at him and smiling, too.

"Jay? Is something happening?"

"I think so," Jay answered, with a hint of laughter in his voice. "I think—"

Suddenly, Unagami's flashlight went out, plunging the cavern into darkness!

"It's just the batteries," he assured Jay. "I'll find some more in my backpack. . . ."

"Don't worry about it, buddy," Unagami heard Jay say. Then the cavern was brilliantly lit by crackling, sizzling energy from Jay's hands! "Like I was about to say, I think my Elemental Power is back . . . I'm the Master of Lightning again . . . in full force!"

But before they could celebrate, a loud rumbling cut him off, and the entire cavern started to shake violently!

"And that sounds like an earthquake," Unagami shouted above the noise, "and it's building to *its* full force!"

## Chapter Five
# Nowhere to Go But Up

"I don't think this is a natural earthquake," Unagami answered, trying to keep his balance. "I think the tribe may have put in some kind of trap to deal with ruin-robbers!"

"But we're not robbing the tribe," Jay protested. Then he realized. "Of course, *they* don't know that."

"We'd better—*Oof!*" Unagami said as a section of the cave's ceiling came loose and struck him on the head. He fell to the ground, limp. More rocks continued to rain down around them.

"Hang on, buddy," Jay said, shutting off the power in one of his hands and scooping up Unagami with it. Then he ran with his friend back to the main chamber, using his powered-up hand to blast away falling debris. Jay saw the stones were getting larger. It wouldn't be long before the cavern was filled— and hopefully, not while Jay and Unagami were in it!

Jay started up the stairs, and as he did, he remembered just how many stairs there were. But all he could do was run up the steps toward distant daylight, firing lightning bolts that smashed large rocks into smaller rocks, then quickly blasting those rocks before they could injure him or Unagami.

It wasn't easy. Jay had to keep track of all the falling stones while also maintaining his balance on the stairway, since there was no railing to keep him from falling off the side and taking the long, long drop back into the rock-choked caverns of the tribe! He slipped once or twice, coming perilously close to falling, and small rocks (some slightly bigger than small) that he hadn't been able to blast pelted him. But he was almost to the surface. He and Unagami were two steps from safety when a massive slab of stone broke loose from the stairway's ceiling

and fell toward them at high speed! Hoping he had enough of a charge left from his lightning powers for a couple last blasts, he smashed the slab in two with one bolt, then pulverized every single piece of debris with a few more! He dashed up the last few steps and collapsed with Unagami in the small clearing. Behind him, he heard a terrible final roar, and when he turned back around, he saw that the entrance to the city was closed—forever.

Jay exhaled deeply . . . and realized he could still feel his Elemental Power surging through him. He swore to himself that he'd never let go of his True Potential again.

"J-Jay?" He heard a weak voice behind him and turned to see Unagami sitting up, blinking. "What happened?"

"We overstayed our welcome," Jay replied, pointing to the rock-filled pit that had been the stairway. "But I followed your advice: I saw a flicker of possibility, so I didn't give in to the darkness. Turns out that even though you're a kid, you do know a few things. Anyway, I think you should have more than enough material for your game. Are you okay?"

"I think so." He looked at Jay with delighted astonishment. "You saved me! Just like one brother would do for another . . . We've formed a bond, like I have with my dad! That makes us . . . family!"

He scampered over and embraced a startled Jay tightly.

Jay was touched, and his voice broke a little when he jokingly replied, "Aw, you're just a kid. What do you know?"

"Am I interrupting something?" Nya asked, stepping into the clearing from the jungle wearing an amused smile.

Unagami, in mid-hug, turned to beam at her. "Jay and I are brothers!"

"Huh?" Nya became very confused when she realized it was Unagami who was hugging Jay.

Jay stood, gently separating himself from Unagami . . . but Unagami wouldn't let go of his hand. Somehow, Jay didn't really mind.

"It's a long story . . . but it ends with me getting my Elemental Power back and feeling a whole lot better about my family"—he smiled down at Unagami—"biological *and* extended."

"That's—that's great!" Nya said, still perplexed, but thrilled for Jay.

"I'm just glad to see you," he said. "How did you find me, anyway?"

Nya smiled slyly as she reached around to pluck something off the back of his belt. Then she wiggled a small device in front of his eyes.

"I planted this little tracker on you when I hugged you goodbye," she said. "I knew you had some things to work out, but I also knew you'd get lost the minute you walked out that door. Your sense of

direction is really horrible. . . . The hotel is just back that way, not very far."

"We all saved each other," Unagami cried, turning to Nya. "Now we're *all* family! Brother, brother, and *sister*! Welcome to the family, Nya!"

Nya smiled, still puzzled but happy. "Thank you," she said. "It's an honor."

"This is great," Unagami exclaimed, taking Nya's hand. "My family is growing every day!"

As they walked toward the brush, Jay looked over Unagami's head at Nya.

"Wait. Is my sense of direction really *that* bad?"

Nya smiled warmly in response. "It's nice to have you back."

# Epilogue

Thank you for allowing me to share the stories of Kai, Zane, Cole, and Jay with you, friend. As you have read, there was no sorcery involved when the ninja regained their Elemental Powers.

Kai needed to accept that he couldn't always be the hero in every situation. And he learned a valuable lesson about the importance of accepting help when it is offered. I confess that I was older than Kai when I learned that lesson myself!

As for Zane—well, he did not hesitate to ask for help in finding his powers. He turned to someone who has helped him many times in the past, and someone he trusts perhaps above all others: P.I.X.A.L. Zane's journey deep into the banks of his fractured memories made him realize that we all need to be able to forgive ourselves for any wrongdoings, or else we can't move forward in life.

A sense of inner peace and wholeness helped Cole and Jay restore their Elemental Powers and True Potential. Giving and receiving strength from your family, and the people you care about, balances and grounds you. Once Cole realized this, the path to rediscovering his True Potential became clear.

Jay's secret to unlocking his True Potential was buried very deep within himself. And he probably wouldn't have been successful without his most unexpected guide, Unagami. The boy helped Jay realize that the family he'd been missing were, in fact, all the people who loved him, cared for him, and stood by his side when he needed them.

When I reflect on these stories, two lessons emerge. First, one can always count on one's friends. And second, no one is ever truly powerless. The stories of others can be instructive in our own lives. Sometimes we can learn something new.

Other times, we can remember something lost that may have been forgotten.

Please come visit me again. Where the ninja are concerned, there are always more stories to tell . . . over a cup of refreshing tea!

Master Wu

# Glossary

## Aspheera

She is a Serpentine sorceress who once stole Kai's Fire power after years of being imprisoned inside a pyramid.

## Cole

Cole was the Earth Ninja and a member of Master Wu's ninja team until he lost his Elemental Power in battle with the Crystal King. Cole is strong and loyal and has sworn to stand up for those who can't stand up for themselves.

### Crystal King

The Crystal King recruited the ninja's most dangerous foes to help him conquer Ninjago. The ninja managed to defeat him but lost their Elemental Powers in doing so.

### Dr. Julien

A brilliant inventor, Dr. Julien created the first Nindroid, Zane, and raised him as his son. Before he died, he shut down Zane's memory.

### Fire Fang

Aspheera created this giant snake to do her bidding. The evil Serpentine sorceress rode it during her attack on Ninjago City. Fire Fang is worshipped by Fire Fiends, humans who live with it in a cave behind the Lake of Fire.

### General Vex

Seeking revenge on a society he believed had rejected him, Vex corrupted Zane and turned him into the evil Ice Emperor. Vex then became the cruel commander of the Blizzard Samurai, known as General Vex.

### Ice Dragon

When Zane overcame his fears and became the Titanium Ninja, he was able to conjure this large elemental dragon.

### Ice Emperor

General Vex erased Zane's memories, and then, with the Scroll of Forbidden Spinjitzu, manipulated Zane to become the Ice Emperor, evil ruler of the Never-Realm.

### Jay

The wisecracking Lightning Ninja used to brighten every situation with his good nature and corny jokes. Adopted as a baby into a loving family, Jay never made peace with being given up for adoption. Since he lost his powers in combat with the Crystal King, Jay has not been his old self and feels he has lost his purpose.

### Kai

Before he lost his Elemental Power, Kai was the brave, hot-tempered Fire Ninja. Now he's confused and trying to rekindle his lost spark.

## Lilly

Lilly was Cole's late mother and the former Master of Earth. Before she passed away, she asked Cole to promise that he would fight for those who couldn't fight for themselves.

## Lou

Cole's supportive father is a stage performer in the musical group, the Royal Blacksmiths. As much as he enjoys performing, he enjoys the time he spends with his son more.

## Master Wu

He is a master of the art of Spinjitzu, which was invented by his father. Wu shares his knowledge with his students—Lloyd, Kai, Cole, Zane, Jay, and Nya—to train them as ninja protectors of the world of Ninjago.

## Milton Dyer

He is the genius who created the *Prime Empire* video game ruled by artificial intelligence called Unagami. He helped end the AI's threat by reaching out to him as he would his own biological son.

## Never-Realm

This distant, wintry realm of Ninjago was once a peaceful, happy place—until Zane became the evil Ice Emperor, and with General Vex, launched a reign of terror.

## Nya

Kai's sister, Nya, a Water Ninja and Jay's girlfriend, is another member of Master Wu's ninja team. She's a voice of reason for the team and a strong source of support for Jay.

## P.I.X.A.L.

Created by tech genius Cyrus Borg to be his assistant, P.I.X.A.L. helped the ninja team. She constructed weapons and tech for them, battled alongside them, and even took over the Samurai-X mech. She is Zane's closest friend.

## Prime Empire

Milton Dyer's complex masterpiece of a multiplayer online game is a world in itself, one the ninja had to battle through and escape while trying to defeat Unagami.

### The Rotten Rabbits

After the ninja lost their Elemental Powers, gangs of roaming criminals—like these bunny-inspired bandits—sprang up all around Ninjago City. They may look tough, but their inexperience means they make a lot of mistakes.

### Sally-Bob

Sally-Bob is an honest, plainspoken farmer whose land is the only thing standing between ruthless Takanagi and his total domination of the region.

### Scroll of Forbidden Spinjitzu

This is one of two scrolls that contains the knowledge of the dark side of the martial art of Spinjitzu. Just touching the scroll gives the holder immense power—and eventually transforms them into a vessel of pure evil.

### Skylor Chen

Her father was an evil crime lord, and her mother was the elemental Master of Amber. Skylor can absorb the elemental power of any other elemental master she touches, but it eventually wears off. She rebelled against her bad father to become an ally of the ninja—and now Kai's girlfriend, too.

## Spinjitzu

This is an ancient technique based on balance and rotation in which one taps into their elemental energy while spinning quickly. Developed by the father of Garmadon and Wu, Spinjitzu is not only a martial art, but also a way of living. Mastering it is a lifelong journey.

## Takanagi

Takanagi is a greedy, ruthless man whose only goal is to get richer by all means possible. He has bought, stolen, and cheated to gain all the land around Sally-Bob's farm. He employs a variety of goons and weapons to try to intimidate Sally-Bob into giving him her land.

## Treehorns

These lanky, creepy creatures look like a cross between a tree and a giant insect. They are fast predators that can quickly overcome and stomp on their prey.

## Unagami

This powerful artificial intelligence tried to take over Ninjago but was stopped by the ninja. After forging a bond with his human creator, Milton Dyer, Unagami transformed into a regular, living young boy.

## Zane

Brave and caring Zane is a Nindroid—a ninja robot—created to protect those who cannot protect themselves, and the former elemental Master of Ice. Before he became the Titanium Ninja, he wore a white uniform and was known as the White Ninja.